"You Want A Child, Don't You?"

Mike sounded a little cool, and warning bells went off inside Joanna's head.

She ignored them. "Yes, very much."

She felt him stiffen, and she knew instantly that she should have paid heed to those warnings. "You don't want children, though, do you?"

"No," he said flatly, "I don't."

She distanced herself from him suddenly and shifted her gaze.

End it now, she told herself. She didn't need the pain and tears that would surely follow.

Only how could she walk away... when she'd just gotten a glimpse of paradise in his arms?

Dear Reader,

Welcome to the merry month of May, where things here at Silhouette Desire get pretty perky. Needless to say, I think May's lineup of sexy heroes and spunky heroines is just fabulous... beginning with our star hunk, *Man of the Month* Cooper Maitland, in Jennifer Greene's *Quicksand*. This is one man you won't want to let get away!

Next, we have the second in Joan Johnston's HAWK'S WAY series, *The Cowboy and the Princess*. Now, please don't worry if you didn't read Book One, all of the HAWK'S WAY stories stand alone as great romantic reads.

Then the ever-popular Mary Lynn Baxter returns with *Mike's Baby* and Cait London appears with *Maybe No, Maybe Yes*. Maybe *you* won't want to miss *either* of these books! And don't pass up *Devil or Angel* by Audra Adams—just which best describes the hero, well, *I'm* not telling. Next, Carla Cassidy makes her Silhouette Desire debut with *A Fleeting Moment*. You'll never forget this witty, wonderful love story.

Yes, May is merry and filled with mayhem, but more important, it's filled with romance... only from Silhouette Desire. So, enjoy!

All the best,

Lucia Macro
Senior Editor

MARY LYNN BAXTER

MIKE'S BABY

SILHOUETTE *Desire*®

™ Published by Silhouette Books New York

America's Publisher of Contemporary Romance

SILHOUETTE BOOKS
300 East 42nd St., New York, N.Y. 10017

MIKE'S BABY

ISBN: 0-373-05781-4

First Silhouette Books printing May 1993

Printed in the U.S.A.

MARY LYNN BAXTER

sold hundreds of romances before she ever wrote one. The D&B Bookstore, right on the main drag in Lufkin, Texas, is her home as well as the store she owns and manages. She and her husband, Leonard, garden in their spare time. Around five o'clock every evening they can be found picking butter beans on their small farm just outside of town.

Prologue

Joanna Nash hummed as she walked toward her car. No matter how bad things were, she thought, her friend Kim always made her feel better. This evening proved no exception. She and Kim had been talking since six o'clock, and now it was after eleven. The lateness of the hour didn't matter; unburdening herself had been good for the soul.

Joanna's humming grew louder at the same time she heard a roaring sound. With her hand on the door of her Honda, she paused, then turned toward the noise.

A fast-driven vehicle had wheeled around the corner and was making its way down the dimly lighted street.

"Jerk," Joanna mumbled under her breath, thinking it was probably some teenager showing off.

She inserted the key in the lock, only to have her breath freeze in her throat. The car, instead of slowing, continued on its fast, destructive path, straight toward her.

Terror flared inside Joanna. Her first instinct was to move, to get out of the way of this lunatic. But the car's offensive headlights rooted her to the spot. It was as if her feet had been cast in cement.

She opened her mouth to scream, but even that reflex failed her. Then it was too late. Her terror suddenly became blinding pain as the car struck her...and she knew no more.

One

―――

"Ms. Nash, can you hear me?"

Joanna fought against the blackness that refused to release her from its icy clutches. Finally she managed to pry her eyes open and focus on the face that leaned over her. A thatch of silver hair above bushy eyebrows filled her vision.

"What...happened?" She licked her dry lips.

"You've been in an accident, and you're in St. Anne's Hospital. I'm Dr. Jason Howard."

Joanna struggled to sit up in the bed, her wide eyes filled with confusion. "An accident?"

"You don't remember what happened?" Dr. Howard asked, a note of concern in his voice.

Joanna took a deep breath, trying to calm her mounting panic. "No," she whispered. "Am I seriously hurt?" Although she felt as though her body had been worked over with a baseball bat, she was able to move at least her arms anyway.

"If you hadn't lunged to the side when you did, you would've been killed."

"Please, what's wrong with me?"

"It's your spine. It's been injured." Dr. Howard paused, and when he spoke again, his voice was even kinder. "You're going to require months of intense physical therapy."

Joanna felt dread seep through her. "How serious is it?"

"You're temporarily paralyzed."

He might as well have put a loaded gun to her head and pulled the trigger. She squeezed her eyes shut while a silent scream threatened to erupt.

"Ms. Nash, look at me."

"Are... are you saying I'll never walk again?" Joanna croaked. Her eyes opened and registered the turmoil raging inside her.

"No, I'm not saying that at all."

"But...but you said I was paralyzed." Joanna tested her lower limbs. No response. She whimpered aloud.

"Now, now, take it easy, my dear. I said 'temporarily paralyzed.' Your injuries are not permanent, nor are they life-threatening. In time, you'll be as good as new."

Joanna fell back against the pillow, her heart racing out of control. She turned and stared out the window and watched as the sun peeped through the blinds. Oh, God, please, let this be a nightmare from which she would soon awaken. Surely this couldn't be happening to her. But it was, she reminded herself, her memory returning with sudden clarity. Clamping down on another urge to scream, she asked, "Who ran over me?"

"Unfortunately no one knows. Hit-and-run, I'm afraid."

Tears brimmed Joanna's eyes. "But why...I can't imagine..."

"I'm sure that's what the police would like to know."

Joanna licked her lips again. "Did Kim find me?"

"Yes, and called 9-1-1. Speaking of Ms. Davenport, she's outside waiting. She's been here all night. Also a detective, Ed Mason, is waiting." The doctor paused and nodded to the nurse who had slipped into the room and was taking Joanna's blood pressure.

When the nurse left, Dr. Howard spoke again. "I'll be back to see you later, and we'll talk more. Meanwhile, is there someone, a family member perhaps, we should contact?"

"Kim will take care of that." Joanna's voice was barely audible.

But it wasn't Kim who came into the room following the doctor's exit. A man, whom Joanna guessed instantly as the detective, strode through the door. He was of medium height with salt-and-pepper hair and a protruding waistline. When he neared the bed and smiled, she knew that he smoked. His teeth were stained a yellowish-brown. But like Dr. Howard, his voice and eyes were kind.

"I'm Detective Ed Mason. I've been assigned to investigate your... accident."

The way he said the word *accident,* as if he'd swallowed something distasteful that had struck in his throat, sounded an alarm inside Joanna. "You sound as if you don't believe it was an accident."

Mason shrugged. "After talking to Ms. Davenport and learning that you're a witness in an upcoming trial, I doubt that it was."

"Are you saying someone could have run me down because they didn't want me to testify?" Joanna heard her voice rise, but she couldn't control it.

"That's exactly what I'm saying."

Joanna flinched inwardly. Could the detective be right? Could the hit-and-run be job-related? She prayed not, but it was a possibility that she was forced to consider.

For several years she had worked as an executive secretary to a savings-and-loan bigwig, only to have the facility collapse and her boss indicted for fraud. The case was due in court soon, and Joanna had been subpoenaed by the government to testify against him.

"I can't... won't believe that someone would deliberately—"

"It happens all the time, Ms. Nash. So until we have reason to believe otherwise, we'll approach it from that angle."

Joanna's eyes fluttered closed. This was too much. She simply couldn't cope with it. She could think only about the chilling prospect that she might not ever walk again. Everything else took a back seat.

Suddenly she ached to be left alone, to nurse her fears in private, to give in to the tears that threatened to choke her. Paralyzed... No! her mind screamed. That couldn't be. Yet she couldn't move her legs.

As if he realized he'd stayed too long, Mason shifted from one foot to the other. "When you're up to it, I need to hear details pertaining to the trial."

Joanna's breath came in quick rasps. "I'll try to organize my thoughts."

"In the meantime, we'll do some checking. You take care. I'll be in touch."

Joanna could only nod and watch helplessly as he shuffled out the door. Twisting her head sideways, she let the pent-up tears flow.

"Do you mind if I come in?"

Joanna jerked her head up, then winced as waves of pain darted through her. She took another ragged breath and slowly let it out. "Oh, Kim."

"Shh, take it easy," Kim said, making her way to the bed where she leaned over and hugged Joanna.

"Oh, Kim," Joanna said again, "I can't believe this is happening."

Kim's blue eyes darkened with sympathy. "You think you can't. When I heard you scream, I thought... Well, it doesn't matter what I thought." She shivered, drawing attention to her overweight body. "All that matters is that you're going to be all right."

"But I might not be," Joanna wailed. She heard the whining note in her voice and fought it. She couldn't let this latest setback defeat her. She was due to start a new job with another successful savings and loan. Though she was highly intelligent and good at what she did, lucrative and challenging jobs were hard to come by. She couldn't lose this opportunity.

"Jo, you've got to think positive, you hear?"

"That's exactly what I've been telling myself, but—"

"Don't say it. Don't even think it." Kim scooped a strand of blond hair off her cheek and shoved it behind her ear. "You have to trust Dr. Howard. He told me that your paralysis is definitely temporary, and that with physical therapy and time, you'll be as good as new."

"But what about my new job?" Joanna asked. So much for the pep talk she'd just given herself.

"What about it?" Kim eased into the chair beside the bed, then scooted to the edge of it. "I'm sure Calvin Granger can make arrangements until you're able to man your desk. After all, he about had a conniption when he thought you weren't going to take his offer. He wants you real bad."

"Let us hope you're right."

"What about your parents? You have to tell them, you know."

Silence fell over the room. At length, Joanna swallowed hard and said, "I know, only I dread it. I can just hear Mother now, especially when I tell her I might be..." She couldn't go on. She couldn't bring herself to say the nasty word *paralyzed*.

Kim frowned. "Nothing's changed between you, then?"

Joanna ran a hand through her tousled chestnut curls. "I'm afraid not." Her mouth twisted into a bitter line. "In fact, I just don't think I can face either of them right now. I need more time."

Not only did she have a huge physical hurdle to jump, she had a mental one, as well. Then again, she had been jumping life's hurdles for twenty-nine years, having grown up as the only child of parents who were so absorbed in each other and their careers as college professors that they ignored her. Her upbringing had been lonely and devoid of loving support. Even today, the crippling insecurities of the past weighed heavily upon her.

"Look, Jo," Kim said a trifle anxiously. "You can't let yourself get down about this. I know what a perfectionist you are, and how you put pressure on yourself to be the very best. And if you do this now, you'll only make things worse."

"Oh, Kim, I'm so scared. What if I don't ever walk again? My life will be over."

"Don't talk like that! If my memory serves me correctly, you said something similar when you lost Megan and divorced Andy."

"That was different."

"No, it wasn't. Andy Lawson was a first class SOB, who would've screwed up your life permanently. Thank God you came to your senses and didn't let him."

Kim was right, Joanna thought. She had fought to salvage her marriage. When she'd finally realized there was no way to do that, she'd filed for divorce.

After college, she had met and married a co-worker, thinking she had found someone who would love her as she longed to be loved. Although her marriage hadn't turned out to be the ideal one she'd envisioned, she had been thrilled when she became pregnant...hopeful that a child would strengthen the relationship. But Andy hadn't wanted a child, and their marriage had taken a turn for the worse.

Despite the marital problems, Joanna had adored the baby daughter she bore, only to stand helplessly by two years later and watch the child die of leukemia.

A week later she'd caught her husband in bed with an old sweetheart. She had filed for divorce immediately, despite her husband's threats to harm her if she went through with the proceedings. Ignoring the threats, she had gone on with the divorce.

Since then, she had poured her heart and body into her work, vowing to never love again. But her secret desire was to do just that. She longed for someone to love her and give her another child. But, fearing those longings would never become reality, she buried them and sought fulfillment in her work.

"Jo?"

Joanna shook her head to clear her mind. "Huh?"

"What did Detective Mason have to say? He asked me some questions, but of course I couldn't help much."

"He thinks the hit-and-run is tied to my work."

"Whew! That's scary. But it doesn't surprise me. Apparently that creep you worked for is capable of anything."

"Well, it surprised me," Joanna said flatly. "And it broke my heart. I thought I'd have that job until I retired."

Kim's lips tightened. "Let's just hope he wasn't behind the hit-and-run."

Joanna shivered, then winced.

"I should get out of here and let you rest. You're in pain, aren't you?"

Joanna forced a smile. "A little. I don't want you to go, but I know you have to." Kim worked as a representative for a New York publisher. Because of that, her hours were more flexible than most. "You've been here all night, haven't you?"

"Yeah, I followed the ambulance. As soon as I sleep awhile, I'll be back with some of your things."

"Thanks, friend." Joanna had trouble speaking around the lump in her throat. "I don't know what I would've done without you."

"Hey, you'd do the same for me." Kim stood, took Joanna's left hand and held it for a second.

"I just hope they get the bastard who did this to you."

"Do you think they will?"

"Yes, I do, especially if it's related to your testimony."

Tears sparkled in Joanna's eyes.

"Hey, don't think about that now. You try to rest. Everything's going to be all right. You wait and see."

After the door closed behind Kim, Joanna stared at the ceiling. Then scrambling to her elbows, she stared at her lower body. Surely she wouldn't lose the use of her legs. She felt as if a giant hand were squeezing the life out of her heart. Hadn't she paid her dues? Wasn't losing a husband and child enough?

She crossed her arms over her chest as silent sobs racked her body.

Two

___

Six Months Later...

The summer afternoon was magnificent. Even though the calendar did say August, the sky was clear, the sun warm, the humidity low.

Joanna was tempted to stop working, walk to the park across the street and soak up the sunshine. The honeysuckle that draped the fence bordering the park was an added seducer. But she couldn't indulge herself. Today was just her second day back at work, and she'd already wasted more precious time than she could afford.

She still couldn't believe it had been six months since she'd been run down in front of Kim's house and her life had changed forever. Yes, she could, she corrected herself mentally, then leaned back in her chair and stared out the window once again. The beauty of the day was forgotten as her thoughts turned to the past months.

When details of the accident reached the papers, friends and co-workers had showered her with flowers, candy and moral support. Because of her preference for privacy, she hadn't realized she had so many friends. While the knowledge had been humbling, it had also contributed to her recuperation. Even her parents had been somewhat supportive.

Yet nothing had had the power to temper the pain and fear endured during those months in hell. Once she'd been dismissed from the hospital, a physical therapist had become her constant companion. And Kim. She would never forget her friend's diligence and determination in making sure that she regained the full and complete use of her legs.

Joanna had fought hard, but there were times when the pain had been so severe that she'd wanted to give up and settle for a wheelchair. Then that inner strength she called on so often had come to her rescue. She'd battled back from the depths of despair and continued to fight.

The worst part had been the complete loss of control over her life. Since the death of her daughter, she had vowed that she wouldn't let things happen *to* her, that instead, she'd make them happen *for* her.

Fate had blindsided her for a second time in her life, and she had been at the mercy of someone else. Now, though, thank God, she had overcome another seemingly insurmountable hurdle, picked up the pieces and started over. She'd never thought she'd ever work again, but here she was back on the job. Only six months, two days and three hours later than she'd planned.

Joanna hugged herself and laughed aloud. To her own ears, the laughter sounded almost strange, especially since there had been so little of it lately.

She looked around her office. It was the size of a postage stamp; still, she was pleased. It connected to her boss's office who was president of the savings and loan. Although she hadn't as yet put her personality stamp on it, the bright orange-and-green decor was quite pleasing on its own.

Joanna turned back to her desk, stared at the stack of folders and grimaced. She'd already plowed through a pile of equal height. She hated to admit it, but she was exhausted. And it was only two o'clock. She also hated to admit that Peter Haskill, her physical therapist, was right. He'd said she needed to strengthen her muscles in order to regain her stamina. The smile died on her lips. She went cold all over at the thought of putting her body through more torture.

"I've gone as far as I can go, you know?" Peter had told her three days ago.

"You mean I have to learn to live with this weak feeling?" she'd asked, appalled.

"Yes, unless you agree to work with a personal trainer."

"A personal trainer?"

"Don't look so disgusted."

"Disgust is an understatement."

"Well, he's what you need to restore the strength to your muscles."

"Are you talking about what I think you are?" she asked, a frown marring her forehead.

Peter grinned; at the same time he shoved his glasses higher onto the bridge of his noise. "Yep. You need to join a gym that has a trainer on staff, or hire him on the side."

Joanna shuddered. "I can't bear the thought. A fitness center is a place I've always avoided. I'm not into sweating."

Peter's features turned serious. "I know, but you don't have any choice." He paused. "I want you to contact Mike McCoy at the Live Well Fitness Club. He's the best." As if sensing her burgeoning displeasure, he added, "I'll go one better. I'll talk to him myself and arrange everything."

Joanna had opened her mouth to argue, only to shut it abruptly. She'd known Peter was right. Still, that hadn't made her decision to comply with his demands any easier. Physical exercise had never appealed to her. Having been blessed with a trim figure, able to eat anything she pleased, she had always sought challenges of the mind rather than of the body.

Now, though, circumstances were different. Pausing in her thoughts, Joanna rubbed both temples.

"Are you all right?"

Joanna looked up and smiled weakly as Calvin Granger walked into the room. Her new boss was tall and thin with graying hair and matching mustache. Although at age sixty-two, he looked like an average American fatherly figure, that image was deceptive. Behind those kind eyes was a sharp mind and a bulldog tenaciousness that wouldn't tolerate anything less than the best from himself or his employees.

That high expectation didn't bother Joanna. Every day of her adult life, she had striven to be the best at what she did. Blessed with above average intelligence, she'd been able to excel.

"Again, are you all right?" Calvin repeated into the silence.

Joanna sighed. "Actually, my head feels like two boxers are slugging it out inside."

Calvin didn't smile. Instead he sat on the edge of Joanna's large desk and scrutinized her. "Maybe you came back to work too soon."

"No, that's not it." She forced another smile. "I think it's the conversation I had with my physical therapist."

Calvin looked puzzled.

"Peter says I should work with a personal trainer, that I'm not as strong as I should be. He suggested a Mike McCoy at the Live Well Fitness Club. Isn't that where you work out?"

"Not only do I work out there, but I'm part owner."

Joanna's eyes widened. "Then you know Mike Mc-Coy?"

"Very well. And I have to agree with your therapist. He's the best at what he does. If anyone can help you, it's Mike."

"If I'm to endure more torture, then I hope you're right."

Calvin chuckled. "I take it you're not looking forward to it."

"I'd rather be shot."

Calvin's chuckle turned into full-blown laughter. "Ah, it won't be that bad. When you regain your weight and stamina, you'll be glad you took Peter's advice."

"Let us pray."

"Why don't I take you to the club this afternoon and introduce you to Mike?"

Joanna barely hesitated. "All right."

"Meanwhile, you go home and concentrate on getting rid of that headache."

"No thanks. Now that I've made a definite commitment to go the personal trainer route, maybe my headache will disappear. Anyway, there's too much work to do."

Calvin stood and gave her an odd look. "You were definitely worth waiting for, Joanna Nash. You're going to be an asset to this company."

Warmth flooded through her. "I'll certainly do my best. Thanks for waiting on me."

"As I said, you were worth it. We'll sneak out around four and head for the gym."

"I can hardly wait."

He laughed again.

The second Joanna walked through the door of the Live Well Fitness Club, she felt her anxiety build, although she had to admit the place was far different from what she'd expected.

Calvin had told her only that the club had moved into new facilities a few months prior. She hadn't been impressed, thinking that old or new, it wouldn't change the fact that it was a smelly, sweat-filled house of torture. She couldn't have been more wrong.

She was greeted by an open reception area with a large circular desk occupying its center.

"Well?"

Joanna turned and gave her boss a sheepish grin. "Why didn't you tell me it was this nice?"

"And ruin your vision of entering a chamber of horrors?"

Joanna flushed. "I can't believe you read my mind."

"Your mind had little to do with it—your expression told all." He paused and stretched a hand in an outward sweep. "So are you impressed?"

"I'm impressed, with the decor that is."

And she was. Her gaze traveled from the teal and salmon colored carpet to the huge exposed steel beams high overhead. In the middle was a round air-conditioning unit. Had it not been painted a bright salmon, it would have been a sore spot.

Lifting her gaze, Joanna took in the second floor that sported a circular track where two people were jogging while looking down on the men's weight-lifting arena.

"Come on, I'll introduce you to the manager. That's him at the front desk."

Joanna followed Calvin to the circular desk that was flanked by plants.

"Tony White, meet Joanna Nash, who's hoping to work with Mike."

Tony, a short beefy man with red hair and a broad smile, stuck out his hand. "It's a pleasure."

Joanna nodded as she extended her hand.

"Do you want to join the club?" Tony asked.

"No, I think I'd rather hire Mr. McCoy on the side, if that's all right?"

"No problem. If I could get you to fill out these papers, we'll be off and running." Tony shuffled through some forms, then handed one to Joanna.

She filled it out quickly.

"Thanks," Tony said, reaching for it.

"Tony, is Mike around?" Calvin asked.

"He's in the back."

"Call him, will you, please?"

"Sure," Tony said, then paged Mike's name over the intercom.

While they waited, Tony introduced her to the two girls who manned the front desk. They didn't bother to mask their curiosity, and Joanna didn't take offense, deciding it was warranted.

First off, she wasn't dressed appropriately. She wished she'd gone home first and changed her clothes. Her lilac-colored linen suit, with its long jacket and perky short skirt, was perfect for the office, but completely out of place here.

While Calvin was in his suit, he didn't seem to garner the stares that she did.

"Come on," Calvin said, interrupting her thoughts. "Let's wait for Mike over there." With a gentle nudge, he prodded her in the direction of the weight-lifting arena. "You'll be working here some, I'm sure, in addition to the special needs room we have specially designed for clients like you."

They had just reached the weights area when Calvin said, "Ah, there he comes."

"Mike McCoy?" Joanna asked inanely, knowing very well who Calvin meant. But she was growing more nervous and agitated by the moment. Regardless of how much physical training would help her, she didn't want to be here. The thought of climbing on any of the machines made her nauseated.

"Mike, it's good to see you," Calvin said, shoving out his hand to the smiling man, who stopped in front of him.

"Likewise, sir." Mike's voice was deep and had a gravelly edge to it.

"I'd like you to meet my secretary, Joanna Nash. I believe her physical therapist spoke to you about her."

Joanna caught her breath as she took in Mike's physical magnitude and cocky good looks. No, good-looking was an understatement. The word *gorgeous* was more appropriate. Dark, unruly hair and black eyes were backdrops for prominent jaw bones, a dimple in the right cheek, and a perfect set of white teeth.

He had a body to match the face. She knew that under his sweats would be a washboard stomach. His buttocks, too, were impressive; they bulged with power. Another detail caught her eye—shoulders as massively proportioned as his buttocks and thighs.

Joanna ripped her gaze away, feeling unnerved by his bigness and muscular strength, a strength that reminded her of her ex-husband and the pain she'd experienced at his hand. She had no use for men who lived by their brawn instead of their brain. They irked her.

"It's a pleasure to meet you," she lied.

Mike's eyes rested exclusively on her, evaluating her with equal boldness. He seemed to smirk as he picked up on her chilly aloofness.

Color stained Joanna's cheeks. She longed to slap that knowing expression off his face. Still, he fascinated her. While there was something bestial and dangerous about him, he was, without a doubt, charismatic from head to toe.

Maybe it was the way he continued to look at her. Her breath caught. Adrenaline rushed through her. Then he turned away, but not before she felt the brunt of his rejection.

She stifled a groan. Working with this man was not a good idea, not a good idea at all.

"Mike, do you think you can help her?" Calvin asked.

Mike faced Joanna again. "It's up to Ms. Nash."

She met his mocking stare. "We can start any time." She wouldn't let him know how he affected her.

"Tomorrow is as good a day as any."

The challenge was there. She heard it in his voice, saw it in his eyes.

Yet the sudden urge to turn and run was so strong that Joanna had to force herself to remain still. "I'll be here," she stated strongly.

Three

———

Mike wiped the sweat from his brow and took several deep lung-burning breaths. He'd finished a boxing match with a friend thirty minutes ago, and still the sweat oozed from his pores. Little good the shower had done him; his body temperature had no choice but to match the weather. So much for the few pleasant days in August. Now it was hotter than hell.

He reached for a towel, and this time mopped his whole face. Tossing the towel aside, he glanced at his watch, then left the men's locker room at the club and made his way toward the training room where he had a cubbyhole office. Once there, he checked the air-conditioning unit and saw that it was already lower than usual.

"You're flashing, McCoy." He chuckled at his own joke before sitting down at his desk and staring at a folder that had Joanna Nash written across it.

No, what had him stirred was his upcoming session with his new client, a session he both dreaded and looked forward to. For him that was a confusing scenario. He'd seen some cold fish in his thirty years, but Joanna Nash ranked near the top, alongside his short-lived fiancée who, like Joanna, had looked on him with contempt. His ex had believed a gym jock like him could never amount to anything, much less make the kind of money he was capable of making. She'd suggested more than once that he should work for her father's bank.

He'd axed that idea along with her, deciding that committing to one person was both risky and painful and that he best not make that mistake again. It was his personal policy to steer clear of the Joannas of the world.

Only, now he couldn't. He'd just have to shrug her attitude aside and resolve to go through with the training. He was committed to his job as an expert with cases like Joanna's. Besides, his helping her was important to Calvin.

Not only was Calvin one of his bosses, but an influential friend, whom Mike hoped would back him with cash for the sports medicine clinic he eventually hoped to open.

Physical fitness had always been Mike's game. During his early years, he had craved outdoor activities because they freed him from the confines of his small, crowded home. One of ten children, he'd grown up poor. But that hadn't embittered him; it had merely made him work that much harder to better himself. Sports became his outlet, the chance he'd needed to beat poverty.

On graduating from high school, he'd boxed on the amateur circuit. The prize money had allowed him to help support his parents and siblings. But he'd longed to go to school, to earn his degree.

Recently he'd begun to realize that dream, thanks to clubs such as this one. His personal trainer's license had been his stepping stone to enrollment at the university where he was working toward a degree in kinesiology.

Nothing was going to interfere with this goal. He'd do what he had to do, even put up with Joanna Nash.

He smiled and shook his head. Yeah, it was a damned shame she was so cold and standoffish. She was one good-looking woman, though. His mind suddenly recalled the details of her face and body. As up close as he'd been, imperfections would have stood out. But he'd seen none—just a cap of short curly hair the rich color of maple syrup, porcelainlike skin, exquisitely formed features, and eyes the color of emeralds. And her mouth—he couldn't forget that. Her lower lip was full, suggesting the potency of her sex.

Too bad it was wasted. Or was it? Maybe underneath that cool veneer simmered a hot fire that merely needed fanning. Suddenly he found himself wondering what she would be like in bed. How would it feel to run his hand over her body, touch her breasts, her nipples? How would they taste? He felt himself grow suddenly and painfully erect.

"For god's sake, McCoy!" His spoken ridicule of himself seemed to have the desired effect. His body relaxed, and he let out a long sigh. Still, his mind wouldn't let go of Joanna—and that would never do.

One of the hard-and-fast rules of his profession was never mix business with pleasure. The Nash woman was definitely business. She needed his help more than anyone he'd seen in a long time. And he wasn't about to let his libido jeopardize his work.

"Hey, Mike, your client is here."

Mike hadn't even heard the door open. He put his wayward thoughts on hold, then smiled at the club manager whose face was withered in a smile.

"When I see someone like Joanna Nash it makes me wish I had your job."

"She's a cold fish," Mike said flatly, Tony's words adding to his irritation.

"Ah, but what fun to warm her up. I'd sure like a shot at it."

Mike looked bored. "Only in your dreams, White."

Tony chuckled. "Want me to send her back?"

"Nah," Mike said, coming around the desk. "I'll go meet her. I want to show her around the club."

Tony grinned. "Have fun."

"Get outta here."

Mike waited several minutes after Tony left before he walked to the front of the club. Joanna stood rigidly by the front desk. It hit him suddenly how forlorn and vulnerable she looked. Then she moved, almost stopping him in his tracks and obliterating everything from his mind except the luscious curves of her body.

"Damn," he muttered, his attention held by the way the black leotards cupped her buttocks, accentuating their taut perfection. The tantalizing did not end there. She twisted sideways, reaching her hand behind her to fiddle with the label on her red tank top. For an instant the silhouette of her high breasts completely filled his vision.

He cursed again, fighting to hold on to his longtime vow *not* to mix business with pleasure. He couldn't cave in now. Still, such feminine perfection seemed a waste of womanhood. Not only was she a knockout, she was sexy to boot—a rare and powerful combination.

She turned then and caught him staring. He saw her stiffen and a veil of hostility darken her eyes.

He glanced away, feeling a flush saturate his face. Damn, he couldn't remember when he'd last let a woman get to him. Nor could he remember when he *cared* that a woman objected to him visually undressing her. The fact that he cared now was what disturbed him.

He took a deep breath, forced a smile, then said, "Hello."

"Hi," she said coolly.

"How was your day?"

"Fine."

So much for polite conversation, he thought, his smile fading. This lady was something else. If possible, she was more uptight than she'd been yesterday. But then, most brainy broads were.

"I thought I'd show you around before we get started."

Her eyes skimmed the premises. "Will I have to work on any of these machines?"

He heard the hesitancy in her voice. Or was it disgust? It made no difference. She might as well know the score up front. "Yeah, you will. Several of them are designed for injuries like yours."

Joanna frowned.

He grinned. "Hey, it's gonna be okay. But you have to trust me. Haskill gave me your workup, and I've been studying it. In no time, we'll have you running the Houston Marathon."

"If that's supposed to make me feel better, it doesn't."

"It will."

"How long will it take for me to rebuild my muscles?"

"Several weeks, for sure."

"I see."

Mike didn't believe that for a second, but refrained from saying so. "Come on, let me show you the lay of the land."

By the time they made it to the training room, Mike felt he'd made some headway in helping Joanna relax. His thinking of her only as client who needed his help and not a desirable woman, whose chilly demeanor he'd like to disrupt, seemed to help.

"Have a seat," Mike said, pointing to the chair in front of his desk.

"Thanks."

"Before we do any exercise, I'd like to go over a few things with you."

Joanna's expression turned suspicious, but when she spoke her tone was even. "All right."

"Your diet is critical to a complete recovery."

"My diet?"

"Don't look so shocked. While you're on an exercise program, it's essential that you eat healthy foods."

"But I do."

The corners of his mouth deepened into a smile. "I think you'll find that you don't, when you take a look at this list." Mike reached into the top drawer of his desk and pulled out several sheets stapled together, then handed them to her.

The room was silent as Joanna's eyes scanned the top page. After a moment she looked up, a ludicrous expression on her face. "You expect me to follow this?"

Mike kept a straight face. "As close as possible."

She shook her head, then gazed back at the page and began to read. "One serving pork and black-bean stir-fry, four radishes, six vanilla wafers, one cup of skim milk."

When she raised her head again, her mouth was set in an obstinate line. "You've got to be kidding. I can't imagine people eating stuff like that."

Mike remained unruffled. "I agree the menus are a little strenuous, especially right now. But I guess what I'm getting at is that you need to be aware of what you eat so that you'll start to regain your strength. It's important that you eat a lot of protein, grains, and veggies."

Joanna smiled. "If I ate like you're suggesting I'd be like a walking skeleton."

"You already are." His eyes roamed over her. "You're much too thin."

Her smile collapsed. The personal comment had suddenly turned a light moment serious. Her face registered a myriad of emotions—embarrassment, fear...

Shifting his gaze abruptly, Mike slammed the drawer shut, then stood. "I guess we'd best get started."

Joanna made no effort to move. Instead she licked her lower lip and asked, "Tell me, do you stick to this diet?"

He felt himself relax, relieved that things were back on solid ground. "Compared to mine, that diet might as well be nachos and greasy cheeseburgers."

"You've got to be kidding."

"I don't kid about something so serious and neither should you. But just to make you feel better, I'll tell you what I had for lunch—raw tuna mixed with lima beans and vinegar."

Joanna made a face. "Yuck."

He chuckled.

"Before the accident, I lived on tacos and cheeseburgers."

He snorted. "If you keep that up, your arteries will be clogged before you're fifty."

"I know, but tacos and cheeseburgers taste good."

He suddenly came from around the desk. "Well...we'd best get started."

Joanna's sigh turned into a grimace.

"Hey, you're not about to be drawn and quartered, you know."

"That's easy for you to say."

He paused, unable to stop himself from again admiring her beauty. Her parted lips revealed small, straight teeth, and her eyes shone with hidden mysteries.

Silently calling himself an idiot, he forced his mind back on business. "We'll meet here in my office every day to go over the planned routine. That'll give me a chance to answer your questions."

"Will I be doing most of my workouts in here?"

They had walked out of his office into the training room itself. Mike watched her as she looked around. He tried for a moment to see the machines and floor mats through her eyes. Although the room was small, it served a purpose, which was to allow private, one-on-one workout sessions, without the distractions of the main gym.

"You'll stretch in here, for sure," he said into the silence. "Then later you'll cool down here. But we'll work both here and in the main gym." Even as he spoke, his eyes scanned the room once again, feeling proud that he had the best equipment in the city. Since such things would mean nothing to his client, he declined to comment.

"Today, we'll begin with only a thirty-minute workout. I want you to do some stretching exercises. In fact, you'll do them every day before we begin. A cool-down will follow. Both are essential. A combination of stretches and limbering exercises gets the muscles warmed and the blood moving, gets them both ready to work. Then the cool-down helps you stretch and relax the muscles you have just worked."

"What happens in between?"

"The treadmill for about ten minutes. That'll get your heart rate up a bit and test your endurance. Then if you're not too fatigued, you can ride the Schwinn Air-Dyne for another ten minutes."

"Is that a bicycle?"

"Yep. Any problems with that?"

She wore an expression of well-chilled distaste, which he decided he'd best ignore. "Watch while I demonstrate the warm-up."

A few minutes later, Joanna had completed the stretching exercises.

"Now, that wasn't so bad, was it?" he asked.

"No, it was worse."

He curbed his urge to throttle her, then pointed toward the treadmill.

The next twenty minutes passed without a hitch. While he sensed that each step on the treadmill and each mile pedaled on the bicycle was difficult, she nevertheless did it, and to his surprise, without comment.

"Time's up."

Joanna mopped her brow with a towel. "What now?"

"Cool-down."

"You mean that's all for today."

"That's all."

Following the cool-down, Joanna took a deep breath. "It's a good thing I'm through. My legs feel like jelly."

"We're gonna take care of that. Lie down on the mat."

Her eyes widened, but she didn't say anything—simply did as she was told. He instructed her through several stretching moves designed to relax her tight muscles. "Feel any better?"

"Not much. My legs are still quivering."

"Maybe this will help. Rest your weight on your elbows, then put you feet together Indian-style."

"What are you going to do?"

Without saying anything, he knelt and placed his hands on her inner thighs. He felt her muscles stiffen. Despite that, he should have continued what he'd set out to do and that was massage her legs.

Only he couldn't. When he realized that his hands were on an intimate part of her and that their breaths were mixing, his hands froze. Hot awareness shot through him, even as that intimacy scared the hell out him.

That was when he made his second mistake. He looked up. The tension suddenly became unbearable. Her eyes were so wide with shock that he felt himself drowning. For the space of a shared moment, they stared at each other.

"I think that's enough for today," he said abruptly, his voice sounding scratchy even to his own ears.

Ignoring the hand he held out to help her up, Joanna scrambled to her feet. "I second that."

Before he could reply, she made her way to the door. Once there, she turned and said, "Er... thanks."

He nodded, then watched helplessly as she shut it behind her. He didn't know how long he stood there with his stomach lodged at the back of his throat.

Four

Joanna knew now why God made Saturdays and Sundays; the working class needed more than one day of rest. Since she had returned to National Savings, her job had been difficult and taxing. Her fatigue, however, was due to the workout session yesterday. In fact, *fatigue* was too mild a word describe how she felt this morning.

She'd awakened early, thinking that she'd get a head start on the day, since her friend Kim was due in and would more than likely want to have dinner together that evening.

Only after she'd tossed back the cover and lifted her legs had Joanna realized that every muscle, every bone ached with a vengeance. She'd fallen back against the pillow and groaned.

Soon she made another effort to move, certain a long soak in warm water and a bubble bath up to her neck would soothe her so that she could walk without wincing. No such luck. The gods had been against her. She did manage to get dressed, though, in a pair of walking shorts, shirt and tennis shoes.

Without so much as a glance at the diet sheets Mike had given her, she'd made her way into the kitchen where she soft-scrambled an egg, buttered a wheat bagel and topped it with raspberry jam. Once she'd gotten something in her stomach, she'd begun her chores. But she'd mumbled a curse with almost every step she'd taken.

Now it was three o'clock, and she was still getting around like an old lady. She was on her way to the couch to rest when the phone rang.

She perched on the arm of the sofa. "Hello."

"Joanna."

"Hi, Mother, how are you?"

"I should be asking you that?"

"Sore, but otherwise fine."

"Sore?"

In her mind's eye, Joanna could see her mother's thin, but attractive, face pinched in a frown. "Yes, sore. *Miserable* is a better word, actually."

"But I thought Peter said you were on the road to recovery."

"He did, and I am, only I started physical fitness training this week."

"Oh, my," Louise Nash said. "Then I suppose it's not a good time for your father and me to come?"

Joanna's felt a sudden surge of joy. Something in her mother's tone was different. Maybe they did want to spend some time with her for a change. "That would be nice. Kim'll be in and maybe we could all go out to dinner."

"Well, why don't you two go ahead and keep your plans. Your father and I can come another time. Anyway, we have a dinner we really should attend."

Joanna's joy turned to despair. She should have known their concern was too good to be true. Suddenly she felt lonelier than she had in a long time.

"That's fine, Mother."

"We'll be in touch. You take care of yourself and don't overdo the exercising."

"Okay."

Once the receiver buzzed in her ear, Joanna fought back the tears. She wouldn't let them do this to her again. Her parents were selfish—always had been and always would be. By expecting more from them, she was only exacerbating her heartache.

She paused in her thoughts and made a face. The last thing she wanted was to dwell on her parents and their shortcomings.

She made her way back into the kitchen of her small but lovely home off Memorial Drive, near her new office. She'd debated about buying another home following the divorce, but in the end, she'd decided that she couldn't pass up the deal on this one.

It was a two-bedroom, two-bath brick that had a big living/dining room with a fireplace. The walls were painted white, which made it seem open and airy. She'd decorated with a salmon and sea-mist green color scheme throughout the house. Plants occupied every available space, taking advantage of the copious sunlight streaming through the large windows. Her dream was to attach a greenhouse onto her breakfast room. One of these days she would have the time and funds to do that.

But for now she had more pressing matters on her mind. She had to live through the workout sessions *and* get through the trial. She faced both with about as much enthusiasm as she would a trip to the dentist.

"You're just one big chicken, Joanna Nash," she muttered as she went to the cabinet where she made herself a cup of gourmet coffee. Acknowledging her cowardice, however, didn't make her feel any better. The only cure for that was to punish her tormentor as he'd punished her.

Mike McCoy was the man with the killer smile and a dimple in his right cheek. Joanna walked into the living room, eased onto the sofa and bit down on her lower lip. She purposefully hadn't thought about *him*. But now that she was, her pulse rate increased. Suddenly she grabbed a pillow and clutched it to her chest. She wouldn't give that big, brawny masochist another thought. Still, the imprint of Mike's perfect body failed to disappear.

So he disturbed her. Big deal. She tossed the pillow aside. She could handle that. She could handle *him*. Couldn't she? Of course, she could. The last thing she wanted in her life right now was a man. But even if the timing was right, she wouldn't want Mike McCoy.

She had managed to successfully bury that other part of her, that sexual being that longed to be held, stroked, loved, that made her so susceptible to heartbreak. She had created that shield around her body and soul with the conviction of a religious novitiate. Since her divorce, there had been few men in her life.

She refused to let Mike McCoy undermine her newfound contentment and purpose in life. Yet never had a man looked at her quite as he had—as though she were the only woman on the planet. She immediately cursed herself for letting that thought slip into her consciousness. His stare wasn't worth a nickel, nor was his attention worth even that pittance. Hadn't she learned from experience that men who were womanizers were nothing but trouble? They didn't have a clue as to how to love or be loved. The McCoys of the world were users.

Then why did her pulse rate skyrocket every time she thought of him?

Swallowing another curse, Joanna sat up suddenly. "Damn," she said, reaching down and massaging the calf of her right leg. Both calves felt like big boils that needed to be lanced.

And the day after tomorrow she would have to go back for more of the same, more pain and more of Mike McCoy.

At first she wasn't sure she'd heard the doorbell, so lost was she in her swirling thoughts.

But when the noise persisted, she realized she had company. Kim. She got up from the couch with as much ease and dignity as she could muster and walked to the door.

"Kim, is that you?"

"Yep."

Joanna yanked open the door, grinning broadly. "Well, it's about time you showed up." She grabbed her friend and hugged her.

When the two women parted, Kim's eyes twinkled. "I've been trying to get here all day, but I went shopping," she announced sheepishly.

"Shopping... You didn't."

Kim dipped her head in mock remorse, then peeked from under her eyelashes, "I did."

"Well, I hope you have a contractor coming to knock out the walls in your closet. I can't imagine where you're going to put another stitch."

"Funny."

Joanna laughed while moving back to let Kim in. Once they were in the living room, Kim swung around and watched as Joanna brought up the rear.

Kim's brows drew together. "What on earth is wrong with you? You're walking like a tree."

"Thanks, friend. You certainly have a way with words."

"Well, it's the truth. So what happened?"

"You don't want to know."

"Oh, yes, I do."

"I had my first workout session yesterday at the gym."

"You, in a gym?" Kim gave a loud whoop. "Why, my stars and stripes, wonders never cease."

"Just shut your mouth and sit down." Joanna's tone was sharp, but her eyes danced. "You want something to drink?" she asked, after they were seated on the couch.

"Nah, not right now, but thanks anyway."

"What time did you get home last night?"

"Around two this morning. The plane was late taking off from N.Y." Kim rolled her eyes. "I'd like it if I didn't have to go to that city. It gets more hectic each time I go."

"You'd best stop griping. Your publisher's never going to move its main office."

"I tried to talk them into moving to Houston, only they didn't listen. Actually, they looked at me as if I didn't have good sense."

"I can't imagine why."

They both laughed, then Kim said, "Well, enough about me. So Haskill finally convinced you that you weren't as strong as you ought to be?"

Joanna shoved her hair behind one ear. "I didn't need convincing, not really. The past few days at the office have been pure hell. I just don't have the stamina I need to do my job. I get unbelievably tired."

"Jeez, if you ask me, you're expecting too much of yourself too soon. Not only was your body brutalized by the accident, but your mind, as well, especially with the police thinking it might not be just a simple hit-and-run."

Joanna sighed. "I know. Coping with all that made me realize I had to regain my strength."

"So Haskill sent you to a club, huh?"

"Yours to be exact."

"Mine? You're kidding."

"Nope, but I sure as hell wish I were."

Kim chuckled. "I can't remember the last time I heard you curse."

"Well, if you'd been around this morning, you would've heard a lot more of it."

"That bad?"

"Worse."

"So who's training you?"

"Mike McCoy."

A ludicrous expression crossed Kim's face. "Oh, boy, oh, boy."

"Exactly what do you mean by that?" Joanna asked in a prim voice.

Kim chuckled that much harder. "I was hoping Dwight Mitchum would've gotten the call."

"Well, apparently Mike's the best, at least that's what Peter and Calvin said."

"Oh, no doubt about that." Kim paused. "Your boss goes to my club. I'd forgotten that."

"He's part owner, actually."

"How about that? So how did you get along with...uh...Mr. McCoy?"

"So you know him?"

"There isn't a female member who doesn't know that hunk."

Joanna felt a sinking in the pit of her stomach, but she chose to ignore it and acted unconcerned. "So?"

"I'm not sure you want to hear the 'so.'"

"If you have anything to say, for heaven's sake, spit it out. I can tell by that Cheshire cat grin on your face that you're harboring a juicy tidbit."

"Not really," Kim said innocently, the grin still in place. "I've just heard that next to physical fitness, women are Mike's passion. Some think he should have a warning label attached to him."

Joanna made an unladylike snort. "Well, this is one who isn't taken in by that . . . that brainless jock."

"Ah, so he's already tried his charm on you?"

"Not exactly," Joanna said, shifting restlessly against the cushion, feeling her face turn red. Then in a disgusted tone, she added, "Who really pays attention to men like him? Oh, I'll admit he's good to look at and seems to have all the right body parts—"

"I'll say," Kim interrupted, her features pinched in a grin.

Joanna ignored her and went on, "But he doesn't interest me, not in the least."

"What I can't imagine is the two of you working together. It's bound to be like trying to mix oil and water."

"That's a good comparison."

Kim slapped her leg. "I knew it. You didn't exactly hit it off, huh?"

"You might say that."

"Well, you'd still best watch your step around him."

Joanna laughed without humor. "You don't have to worry about me. I got his number from the start. Besides, men like him leave me cold."

"Methinks you're protesting too loudly."

Joanna suddenly reached for a cushion and tossed it at Kim. "Some friend you are."

"I know." Kim grinned. "Look, I'm starving. Let's go eat. While we're at it, I'll tell you about a new aerobic exercise you might like to try."

"I wouldn't count on it, if I were you."

Five

Kim stepped off the bench and glanced down at her watch. "I can't believe it. Are you really here, or are you a figment of my imagination?"

"Shh, Kim, not so loud," Joanna said between clenched teeth, taking in the curious stares from several women standing on the aerobics floor.

Kim's grin held no remorse. "Why? You ought to be proud of yourself."

"One of these days I'm going to put a knot on your head."

Kim looked repentant. "I wouldn't blame you if you did."

She then stepped off the floor and joined Joanna on the sidelines. Joanna had half promised Kim that she'd come to the club this morning, which was Saturday. Kim had insisted on showing Joanna the latest in the

aerobics phenomena—working off steps or benches.
The workout had already taken ten pounds off Kim.

"The class is due to start in about fifteen minutes."
Kim stretched her arms over her head. "Can you stay
and watch?"

"For a while. I thought I'd go to the office and work
some, then go see my parents. They've been wanting to
come see me, but I'd rather go there."

"Think you could ever get into this?" Kim pointed
toward the floor and watched as the instructor posi-
tioned their benches in preparation for the class. "Not
for the purpose of losing weight, of course, but for
stamina?"

"Not me," Joanna said flatly.

Kim's lips turned down. "Didn't think so."

Joanna didn't respond. Instead her eyes roamed the
premises. It was a gorgeous summer day, though extremely hot. Inside the club it was pleasant; muted
sunlight poured through the huge skylight in the ceiling and bathed the room in its soft glow.

The club swarmed with men and women pumping
iron. She smiled to herself. While it was a fact that the
physical fitness wave had swept the country, there was
more to it than that. Swim season was in full swing,
which meant better bodies and dark tans.

Joanna's eyes rested on the men's free-weight section. It was then that she saw him. He had just placed
a heavy weight back on the rack, looking completely in
his element. From where she stood, she could see the
sweat on his face, but it didn't detract from the rugged
perfection of his face and body. He moved to another

rack, walking with the loose grace of a healthy animal.

"Gorgeous, isn't he?"

Joanna flushed at having been caught staring at Mike. "I've seen better looking."

Kim harrumphed. "Not in this lifetime, you haven't."

"Men like Mike McCoy leave me cold."

"Hmm . . . he looks like a boxer, don't you think?"

Joanna frowned with a shudder. "Now, that's a sport I can't tolerate. Why anyone would want to punch another human until they knocked him out is beyond me."

"I don't happen to like it myself, but to some, I'm sure it has its pluses."

"Mike McCoy for one."

As if he sensed that he was being scrutinized, he looked their way. Joanna's gaze connected with his. For a moment the room spun, and the blood raced through her hyped-up body.

He simply nodded, replaced the second weight and began walking toward them.

"Uh-oh, here he comes," Kim whispered.

Again Joanna's pulse accelerated with a purely female response. Then her sound judgment came to her rescue, turning that awareness into irritation that bordered on anger. This easy-walking jock with his knowing eyes and his powerful body could not be trusted.

With this thought in place, she fought to keep her emotions at bay. She must remember that he was nothing more than her trainer, and when she was whole, she'd never see him again.

"And wouldn't you know, I gotta go." Kim nudged Joanna on the arm. "The class is starting again."

Joanna swung around. "Don't you dare leave me," she said through clenched teeth.

"I have to. Besides, you're alone with him for what—three days a week? You might as well toughen up now." She nudged Joanna on the arm and winked. "Try not to let him bite."

Joanna would have loved to punch her friend on the spot. But before she could even reply, Kim scooted off. Out of the corner of her eye, she saw Mike continue to thread his way toward her.

He finally stopped within touching distance, his expression as cloaked as hers. "Hi."

Her heart pounded in her throat as she looked once again into his eyes. "Hi."

"I have to say I'm shocked to find you here this morning."

"No more shocked than I am to be here."

He lifted his eyebrows, as if to say, "Why are you, then?"

Joanna sucked in her breath, only to get a whiff of his hot body. She wanted it to be a turnoff, but it wasn't. She swallowed hard. "Kim twisted my arm."

"Kim Davenport?"

Joanna nodded. "She's a friend, who's a firm believer in exercise and this club."

"And she's trying to convince you to get on the bandwagon?"

"Something like that?"

"Only it's not working?"

"What do *you* think?"

"Even if you were a hundred percent fit, a blast of dynamite couldn't get you out on that floor."

"That's right."

Mike smiled that killer smile. "Oh, by the way, how's the diet?"

Joanna wrinkled her nose. "Just exactly as you think it is."

He laughed again. "Well, you can't blame a person for trying."

She smiled in return, and for a moment they were silent, as if they had suddenly run out of anything to say. But the tension between them was no less tense. They continued to stare, and for a moment it seemed as if both were oblivious to the people and the noise around them.

Joanna cleared her throat and was about to force herself to say something, anything that would break the spell, when Mike shifted his gaze and spoke. "Well, I see my 10:40 client coming. I guess I'll see you Monday."

"Guess so," Joanna muttered, also keeping her eyes averted.

He opened his mouth as if he wanted to say something else, but he didn't. He shut it abruptly, then turned and walked off.

Joanna hadn't realized she'd been holding her breath until her chest began to feel as if it would explode. Damn, she was going to have to get control of her emotions. Control. That was the key. She couldn't remember when they had been so *out* of control. But there was something about this gym jock that turned her inside out.

"Hey, are you on your way out?"

Joanna turned and smiled at Kim, who stood beside her, sweating profusely. "Is the class already over?"

"No," Kim said, fighting for her next breath. "The instructor's just giving us a short water break."

"Sounds like you need it."

"No pain, no gain."

Joanna pursed her lips. "Spare me."

"Call me, okay?" Kim said with a grin.

"Okay."

"Oh, before you leave, is there anything you want to tell me?"

"Such as?"

Kim grinned. "Like what you and Mike were so deep in conversation about?"

Joanna felt her face turn red, and she hated it. "Besides being nosy, you're conjuring up all sorts of things that just aren't going to happen."

"Maybe. Maybe not. Obviously you haven't picked up on the way he looks at you."

"Go on, get back to your workout."

Kim's grin widened as she dashed back to the floor.

Joanna sighed, then turned and headed toward the door, her mind churning with unanswered questions.

"I'm sorry, but Mr. Granger's out of the office today. I can make an appointment for you tomorrow."

Joanna listened to a whiny monotone on the other end of the line with little patience.

"I'm aware that your time is valuable, Mr. Edwards, but so is Mr. Granger's."

She listened a bit longer, then hung up, but only after the man decided that he'd go elsewhere to do business. She lowered her head in her hands and massaged her temples, wishing that days like today could be outlawed.

Since she'd arrived at her desk at seven o'clock this morning, the phone had not stopped ringing. It was now after one o'clock, and she still hadn't made a dent in the work piled on her desk.

She thumbed through the top files, noting that she had at least five loan documents to prepare in addition to several important letters to type.

What she'd have *liked* to do was get out of what she absolutely *had* to do, then go home and take a long soaking bath. Instead, she had to go to the gym and face a grueling workout . . . and Mike McCoy.

If only he didn't have to put his hands on me.

Joanna stood abruptly as if the action would relieve her thoughts. She turned and walked to the window just as she heard the knock on her door.

"Come in," she said without turning around, thinking it was one of the other secretaries.

"Good morning, Ms. Nash."

The gruff voice of Detective Ed Mason brought her around with a start. "Hello," she said with reservation. What did he want?

The corners of his mouth twitched into a smile. "Maybe I should say afternoon."

Joanna smiled weakly. "Whatever."

"Do you have a minute?"

"Of course. Please, sit down."

Joanna watched as he hitched his wrinkled slacks and slouched into the chair in front of her desk. She almost smiled, thinking that in appearance, he fit Colombo to a T. Yet she knew this was no bumbling, fumbling detective, but a sharp, intelligent one, who missed very little. And that was why she stiffened. Something was up, or he wouldn't be here.

"Have you had any contact with your ex-boss's attorney?"

"None."

"Anyone else contact you?"

"Only the assistant D.A.'s office."

"That doesn't surprise me."

"What are you getting at, Detective? Surely you don't still think the hit-and-run is job-related?"

"Yes, ma'am, I do."

Joanna sighed, sat down in her chair, then said with firm conviction, "Well, I don't."

Mason toyed with his mustache for a moment while watching her closely. "We're in the process of checking several repair garages around the area."

He waited for her response and when there was none, he went on, "A plainclothesman has been assigned to your house."

"What?"

"It's for your protection."

Joanna's head pounded. "But I don't want anyone to watch me or my house."

"I'm aware of that, but my boss thinks it's the way to go until we know for sure."

"Are you trying to frighten me, Mr. Mason? If you are, you're doing a good job of it."

"That's not our intention. But at the same time, we have to do what we think best."

"All right, but I don't like it."

Mason stood and ran his fingers through his hair. "I know, and we'll try to be as scarce as possible."

When he shut the door behind him, Joanna felt her frustration level reach an all-time high. No arrangement was going to suit her.

Six

"When will you and Daddy be back?"

"In about a week," Louise Nash responded.

"I don't guess I'll see you till you come back, then."

"No, there's just not time."

Joanna heard the impatience in her mother's voice but tried not to let it bother her. Only it did. She'd be damned, though, if she let it show or if she'd let her mother off the hook so easily.

"Well, I'm sorry we didn't make connections this past weekend."

Louise's profound sigh into the receiver didn't escape Joanna's ears. "I know, honey, and I'm sorry about that, too. But you know your father and his work. When Professor Adams asked him to chair that fund-raiser dinner, he couldn't very well turn him down."

"I understand, Mama," Joanna lied, trying desperately to keep the forlorn note out of her voice.

"Of course you do. You always have. Oh, by the way, have you heard any more about the accident?"

"No, no I haven't. The police are still investigating from the angle that it was job-related."

"My, I certainly hope not."

"Me, too."

Silence.

Joanna ignored the burning sensation at the back of her eyelids and said, "Well, you be careful, and I'll talk to you when you get back."

There was a short silence, then Louise said, "You're taking care of yourself, aren't you?"

"Yes, Mother." If her mother heard the trace of sarcasm in her voice, she chose to ignore it.

"We'll talk to you later, then."

When Joanna replaced the receiver, she stared into space for a long moment—so much for the concern her parents had shown following the accident. Now that she was back to work, they assumed that she was back to normal.

If only that were the truth. She feared her life would never be back to normal. Ed Mason had certainly done his part to add to the confusion and frustration boiling within her. She didn't want to think that someone might be out to get her. The thought was so absurd, she couldn't think about it without smiling.

Granted, Tom Hancock, her ex-boss, was enraged at being arrested. But that didn't mean that he had the guts or the wherewithal to threaten her life if she testified against him.

Still, she had to comply with the law.

Joanna smiled suddenly, only to have that smile turn into a frown. She needed protection all right, but not from some unknown force that might or might not be lurking about her. The protection she needed was from that brainless jerk in the gym.

"Give it a rest," she muttered, even as she shed her clothes and donned her workout clothes. She wouldn't let him unnerve her, not anymore. She'd ignore the spear of longing that never failed to shoot through her when he looked at her in that special way, as if he alone knew the secrets of her body. It was only a matter of controlling her hormones and squashing her desires.

With that pledge uppermost in her mind, Joanna grabbed her purse and headed out the door.

"Why can't I see you tonight?" Tanya Hall whined, her huge eyes tracking Mike's every move.

Mike suppressed a sigh as he laid down the barbell, then sauntered back into his office, all the while mopping sweat from his face. The more he wiped, the less good it did. Disgusted, he tossed the towel aside and turned his attention to the blonde whose shapely hip rested on the edge of his desk.

"I told you I was busy."

"You're always busy," she whined, "or at least you have been for the past two weeks."

"Look, Tanya..."

She held up her hand. "I know. I know. You don't want me to pressure you."

"That's right."

The pout of her heavily glossed lips intensified. "But I thought we had something going."

Mike held his silence while his eyes raked her. What he saw, he liked. She had a nice shape—a tiny waist and great legs. And she was crazy about him. So what was his problem? Ordinarily, he'd be doing his best to pursue this relationship.

But that was before he'd met Joanna Nash. For the life of him, he couldn't figure out why she'd put a crimp in his hormones.

"Mike?"

He shook his head. "Sorry."

The pout stretched into an angry line. "Have I done something?"

Mike shook his head. "No, Tanya, it's not you—it's me. I'll call you, okay? Let's just leave it at that."

"Fine." She lunged off the desk and flounced to the door. "But you won't call, and we both know it."

His eyes narrowed at the change in her voice.

"Who is she?"

"I don't know what you mean."

"Like hell you don't. I may look like a bimbo, but I'm not." With that, she walked out the door and slammed it behind her.

Mike swore at the same time he felt the room rock. Women. They were nothing but trouble. Joanna Nash in particular. Suddenly he longed to escape to the gym where he boxed. Punching the bag had the power to relieve his frustrations.

But even that labor of love wouldn't be enough to keep his mind off Joanna and their upcoming session.

He couldn't remember when a woman had played such havoc with his life.

What was there about her? He wasn't sure. Her image was forever with him, always tormenting him, forever forcing him to ask questions that had no answers . . . questions such as: How would it feel to hold her, to touch her, to bury himself deep inside her?

And why the hell did he give a tinker's damn? His taste ran more to the Tanyas of the world. In fact, he'd always made it a point to steer clear of women like Joanna. She was too uptight, too intellectual to suit him, too perfect, for god's sake.

Yet he couldn't stop thinking about her or wanting to touch her.

He lifted the barbell again and pumped it for all it was worth.

"Hello."

Mike's hand froze, and he whipped his head around. He blinked the sweat out of his eyes, then raked them over Joanna as she stood inside the room.

She had on black tights that hugged her legs, a yellow tank top and an oversize silky white shirt. Her hair was swept away from her face into a tumble of curls. The fragrance of that hair perfumed the air. He breathed deeply, so as to draw the smell deep into his lungs.

"Shall I come back later?" she asked.

Joanna's chilly tone of voice hit him like a douse of cold water. He swore silently while easing the barbell onto the rack.

"No. You're right on time. I'm the one who's running late."

Sweat glistened on his chest. He saw her eyes dip there and remain. Only when he shoved a hand through his hair did her head bounce back up. Her face was flushed, and if he wasn't mistaken, he'd seen unconscious hunger in her eyes. Only now she refused to meet his gaze. Good, he thought childishly. She wasn't as immune to him as she'd have him believe.

"Are you feeling any stronger?" he asked before the silence became unbearable.

"A little."

"Did you work all day?"

Joanna's face brightened. "Yes, for the first time since the accident."

"Great." He tossed the towel over the rack, reached for his T-shirt and slipped it over his head.

She didn't say anything. Instead, she removed her shirt, then folded it into her bag. This time it was he who stared at the way the cotton top adhered to the full curves of her breasts. A shaft of hot desire charged through him, rendering him useless for a moment.

He cleared his throat, yet his voice was thick as his eyes focused on her hair. "Today you're going to work out on some of the machines out front, specifically the leg extender and the leg curl."

"Whatever you say."

"Try not to get so excited." He meant for her to pick up on the sarcasm in his voice and she did. She tensed instantly. He drew a deep breath. It was going to be another one of those days. He felt it in his bones.

"Ready." He pointed toward the door.

She nodded.

"Let's get to it."

He followed, and couldn't help but notice the hypnotic swing of her trim hips. By the time they reached the designated area, his breathing was labored. He was sure she hadn't noticed. Her concentration seemed to be on the people working out as well as the aerobic dance class that was in full swing.

He didn't speak again until they reached the first machine. "Okay, here's the way this works."

Joanna looked on as he climbed onto the machine and demonstrated.

He smiled, but elicited no response from her. She focused on the barbell with an intensity that was almost tangible. "It's your turn," he said.

After she'd done two sets, he stopped her. "How do you feel?"

"Shaky, but all right."

"You want to stop?"

"No."

"Good girl."

She completed the sets on both machines. But it wasn't easy. Her breath came in short spurts, and a fine sheen of sweat dotted her forehead.

"I think we'll give your upper arms a shot today as well. Let's go back to the training room. The ladies small-arm machine is in there. It's much quieter in there." He turned toward the aerobic area. "Damn, but that music's loud."

"That it is."

The room was empty when they entered, and Mike was thankful for that. Joanna didn't need any distractions. Briskly, and in his most businesslike tone, Mike crossed to the rack lined with small dumbbells and lifted one.

"This is what I want you to do. Watch." He moved his arm in a curling motion, in and out.

Once the five-pound dumbbell was in Joanna's hand, she followed his example.

"Hurts, huh?" he asked, after watching her wince.

"Like someone is sticking needles in my arm."

"That's because you're not doing it exactly right."

Her lips tightened, and she gave him a scathing look.

Mike ignored her. "Concentration is the key. You have to concentrate so that you won't just swing your arms. The movements have to be controlled. Here, I'll show you again." He grabbed a dumbbell off the rack and demonstrated the tricep and bicep curls.

"I thought that was what I was doing."

"Give it another shot, okay?"

Her eyes glittered. "No."

He drew in a harsh breath as he looked at her and watched perspiration appear from her scalp and run across her brow into her eyes. She blinked them back. Suddenly he noticed the stark line of fatigue—or was it tension?—around her eyes and mouth. He felt a pang of guilt, but guilt was not what she needed. She needed his strength. "What do you mean, no?"

Her chin jutted. "You figure that out."

He made a choking sound. He hadn't lost his temper in a long time, but he was perilously close to it now. His head pounded, and he hadn't slept in Lord knows how long, and she was watching him as though he was about to do some unthinkable harm.

"Look, your mind isn't on this today," he said, his voice no longer soothing. "And we both know it."

She shifted her gaze. "I'm just tired."

"That's not the real reason. We both know that, too."

Their working together simply was not *working*. He'd never had a hostile client before, and frankly he was at a loss as to how to deal with one. He was attracted to her, which he figured was the whole damn problem. Because his charm *hadn't* worked on Joanna, it both frustrated and intrigued him. Yet he had a job to do and nothing was going to interfere—certainly not his libido.

"What are you saying?" she asked in a voice too high and thin.

"I'm saying that this isn't working out, that you're not cooperating."

"Maybe you're right."

It wasn't so much what she said as the way she said it that alerted him. She wanted him to end these sessions, to say they shouldn't work together anymore. He could see it in her eyes and in the expectant way she seemed to hold her breath.

Like hell. He'd made a commitment to help her, and he damn well wasn't going to renege on it. Besides, she *needed* his help. Just as he'd explained to her several times already, he was the best trainer around when it came to her type of injury.

"I'm not letting you off the hook," he said coldly, "if that's what you're hoping to accomplish. You're paying me to do a job, and I'm going to do it."

"I could fire you."

"Yeah, you could."

He stepped closer. "But you won't, will you?"

The silence was startling.

Her tongue moved across her lower lip, wetting it. He didn't move, giving his sudden and fierce arousal time to subside.

As if she'd read the blatant desire in his eyes, she sucked in her breath. The air vibrated with suppressed sexual tension.

"Well?"

Another silence.

"No...no...I won't fire you," she said in an unsteady whisper.

Seven

What was wrong with her? She knew the answer, though vehemently tried to deny it. Mike McCoy was the *who* that was wrong with her rather than the what. Throughout the week, Joanna had caught his eyes in a critical examination of her body. The invasion of privacy had been aggravating, yet exciting, too.

And if thoughts of *him* weren't enough to keep her on edge, there was the plainclothes detective, who, despite Mason's promise of anonymity, continued to be a thorn in her side. Whenever she walked out her door, backed out of her driveway, there he was, watching. Not only did his presence unnerve her, but it angered her, as well. Maybe if she'd had threatening phone calls or been approached by someone asking questions, his concern might have been warranted. Nothing, however, had happened to make her think that the hit-and-run was not an accident. And she resented the police making it into a possible life-threatening scenario.

She did have one thing to cheer about—each day she enjoyed her work more. Apparently her boss was pleased because she'd already received a raise in salary. On the other hand, Calvin didn't seem as confident about her physical state. He persisted in worrying about her.

"Is Mike's exercise routine doing the trick?" he'd asked just that morning.

"I honestly don't know," she'd said, wincing as she'd made a sudden move.

Calvin raised his eyebrows. "Seems to me you're awfully sore. After two weeks, you should be over that, shouldn't you?"

"Mike assures me that someone with my type of injury will feel the effects of exercise much more than someone who's simply toning her muscles."

"That's why I don't want you to tax your strength here at the office."

Joanna smiled. "Don't worry. I won't push myself beyond my limitations. I promise."

"I don't believe that for a minute. But it sounds good."

Her eyes twinkled. "It does, doesn't it?"

That conversation had taken place just that morning. Now she was getting ready to go to the club.

"Urggh!" she said as she struggled into her black tights, long cotton T-shirt and Reeboks. By the time she was dressed, her mood had worsened and she was feeling sorry for herself.

God, but she was sore. How much longer was this torture going to last? she wondered, her mind conjuring up ways she could torture Mike in order to repay him for the misery he was putting her through, both physically and mentally.

She smiled without humor, even as the image of his body once again rose to the forefront of her mind. She bet she could hit him in his washboard stomach with a baseball bat, and he wouldn't so much as grunt.

She felt her face grow warm, her mind refusing to let go of that image. While his body in itself was a work of art, everything else about him intrigued her, as well. His dimpled smile, the puzzled looks in her direction, the touch of his hand.

Her reaction to his touch was what disturbed her the most. She should have feared him. The fact that he was so big, so muscular should have been the catalyst to force her distance. Only it hadn't. For his size, his touch had been gentle. When he'd placed his hands on the inside of her thighs, she'd melted inside.

Irritated at the avenue her thoughts had taken, Joanna looked at the clock on the table beside her bed and made a face. If she didn't get a move on, she'd be late. No big deal. But the sooner she got to the club, the sooner she'd get through her workout. Aside from the fact that she wasn't Mike's only client, she believed in punctuality.

Visions of an eventual long soak in the Jacuzzi, followed by a cup of gourmet coffee provided her with the incentive to get up and walk out the door.

* * *

As usual, when Joanna walked into the club, it swarmed with people and the music blared. She wished she enjoyed this physical shock to the body as others seemed to. Maybe one of these days...

"Hi, Joanna," Tony said from his position behind the desk.

"Hello."

"How's it going?"

Joanna's mouth turned down, especially as she felt his admiring gaze sweep over her body. "I'll let you know, after my session."

Tony chuckled. "Hey, it's going to be all right. Trust me."

Joanna shook her head. "You physical buffs are all alike. The more pain you inflict on yourselves, the better you like it."

"Ah, now who told you that?"

"Where's Mike?" she asked, ignoring the lingering warmth in his voice and eyes.

"Hold on. I'll page him."

"No, don't. I'll just wander back toward his office. I'm sure he's expecting me."

"See you later."

Joanna made her way down the middle of the machine section just as Mike was coming toward her. An emotion she couldn't quite read leapt into his eyes. Yet it gave relief to the tired, drawn look around his eyes. Just as quickly, his lids shuttered and the emotion was lost.

He stopped within touching distance and asked,

"Are you ready to get started?"

"Yes."

"Ten minutes on the NordicTrack is the first order of the day."

He took a step back, and she released her pent-up breath, though her pulse refused to settle. "Let's get it over with."

For the next forty-five minutes, Joanna worked herself into a sweat. Only after she laid down a dumb-bell, did he look at her close enough to see her wince from a sudden jab of pain.

"What's wrong?" Mike's tone was rough, but his eyes were dark with concern.

"I thought I was getting a cramp in my leg."

"A charley horse."

She nodded in the affirmative.

"Okay now?"

"I think so."

He stared at her for a moment. "I think you've had enough for today."

"Are you serious?"

His mouth twisted into a half smile. "Don't get too excited. We're not through yet."

Joanna's face fell. "Oh."

He laughed and her breath unraveled. "Nope. You're not going to get off that easy."

"So what now?"

"The whirlpool."

She blinked at the same time her heart skipped a beat. "Whirlpool?"

"We need to knock that swelling in those joints. We'll go from ice-cold water into hot."

Joanna gasped. "Now?"

"Now."

She didn't move.

"Go on. Put on your bathing suit. You do have it, don't you?"

"Yes," she said in a small voice.

There was a pause. "What are you waiting for, then?"

Swallowing a frustrated scream, Joanna headed for the ladies' change room. Even after she'd slipped into her bathing suit and taken several deep breaths, she didn't feel a bit better about the sudden turn of events. With a robe shielding her, ignoring her thudding heart, she walked into the designated area.

Mike stood waiting for her. She pulled up short. He, too, was dressed in swim gear, only his body wasn't covered. While she'd imagined what he'd look like under his clothes, the real-life version was even better than her fantasies.

From his neck to his feet, his body was rock-hard. Dark hair matted his chest and didn't stop until it reach the band of his trunks. She didn't let her eyes dip any farther for fear of what she'd see. Still, she felt the color flood her cheeks.

"Ready?"

Did his voice sound gravelly or was it just her imagination? But when she chanced a look in his direction, his lips were twisted slightly. Her cataloging of his body hadn't gone unnoticed. Damn him. "Ready as I'll ever be."

He held out his hand, indicating she should go first.

Joanna hesitated, hating to discard her robe and subject herself to the same scrutiny she'd given him. He wasn't about to turn his head, either.

Without looking at him, she slowly slipped the garment off her shoulders. She heard the faint sound of his indrawn breath at the same time she felt his eyes on her body. Even though she'd lost weight, she knew she could be proud of how she looked in a bathing suit.

Joanna met his stare, conscious of the clamoring it created within her.

"You have a great body," he said thickly.

She licked her cotton-dry lips. "Thank you."

Their gazes held for another moment, then he said, "Go on, get in."

She did as she was told and stepped into the small pool filled with cold water. "Brrr," she said, shivering.

Mike squatted down on one knee by her side. "Walk around a bit, then you can get out."

Moments later, she was out of the cold and into the warm. "Ah, that feels better," she said, resting her elbows on the side of the bubbling whirlpool.

"Good. Now for the workout." Mike stepped onto the first step.

Joanna froze. "What are you doing?"

He stopped. "What does it look like I'm doing? I'm getting into the pool."

She should've seen this coming. She would have if she hadn't been so struck by his near-nude body. Why else would he have put on his swim trunks? Still, she heard herself stammer, "B-but . . . why?"

"Why? To massage your muscles. You have a problem with that?"

Her knees turned so weak that they barely supported her. "Is . . . that necessary?"

He smiled without humor. "Yeah, it's all part of the healing process."

"I . . . can massage my own muscles."

"No, you can't." Impatience colored his tone.

Once he was in the water, he said, "Sit on the step and extend your legs."

He worked on her right one first. The instant he placed his hand on her naked leg, an electrical charge surged through her. She jumped, but he didn't stop. Everywhere his fingers touched, they seemed to burn her flesh.

Sheer force of will kept her from squirming, for she was no longer afraid of being touched by this strong man. Suddenly she ached to touch him as he was touching her. She had read an article in a magazine about women's sexuality, which had stated that the skin was the body's largest organ, that it was an erogenous zone, full of nerve endings and extrasensitive areas, all tremendously important when it came to sexual stimulation. She hadn't believed it then, but now she knew what she'd read was true.

"You're too tense," he muttered. "Relax."

Relax! How could she relax when he was using his hands as erotic appendages? He started at her toes and worked his way upward, gently massaging, kneading . . .

"I'm trying," she said at last, hearing the tremor in her voice, and knew he did, too.

When his hands worked their way to her shoulders, she thought she couldn't handle it, especially as his face was so close to hers.

"That's it," he said, his breath striking her cheek in a soft, ripping sound.

She looked at him then. The atmosphere suddenly turned thick and heavy. He was so close, she could see the fine lines around his eyes. He edged his face nearer. Her heart stopped. Was he going to kiss her?

He cleared his throat and pulled back. "I think that's enough for today."

His tone was brusque, and he shifted his gaze, but not before Joanna saw the cold glint that had replaced the fire in his eyes. Her heart thudded back to life as color flooded her face. Apparently he wasn't pleased with this sexual awareness between them. She wasn't, either, of course. Somehow that gave her the comfort she needed to put her legs into action. She climbed out of the whirlpool and turned her back.

"Joanna."

She stopped and swung around, feeling the color in her face deepen. "Yes?"

"Can you tell any difference in your muscles?"

Again she was caught off guard. His face and voice were all business, bearing no resemblance to the tortured man of a moment ago. "A hundred percent," she said, forcing a coolness into her own tone.

"Good. I'll see you after you change."

She walked out of the room without saying anything.

"Gotta a sec to spare?"

Mike turned his back on the window and stared at

Tony, whose lean frame barely filled the doorway. "What's up?"

"Has Joanna left?"

"She's in the dressing room."

Tony rubbed his chin. "How's she doing?"

"Fine."

"Boy, you're in a talkative mood, aren't you?"

"I've got a lot on my mind."

"It wouldn't have anything to do with Joanna, would it?"

"That's none of your damn business." Mike's tone was cold and flat.

Tony shrugged with a grin.

"So what do you want?"

"We're going to do some TV commercials in an attempt to derail our newest competitor."

"Lance Newlin, right?"

"Yep. I got the word this morning."

"Damn," Mike said, his thoughts switching to his one-time sparring partner who had recently come into some money and had decided he could switch overnight from an unsuccessful gym rat into a successful businessman. Mike knew better, or at least he hoped so. Two fitness clubs within striking distance of each other could mean the kiss-of-death to both. The way he figured it, only the survival of the fittest, literally, would make it. He was hell-bent on making sure Live Well was the survivor.

Tony shuffled his feet. "Of course, it's gonna be a while before they're ready to open, especially with all the rain we've had. Still, I want to take away as many prospective clients as I can."

"Right, but why don't you let Morrison do the commercials? Damn, man, I don't have time. School's eaten my proverbial lunch, as it is."

"I know, but you've done it before."

"Oh, all right." Mike's tone was resigned. "I'll do it this time, but no more."

"Gotcha."

When Tony eased out of the doorway, Mike glanced at his desk and groaned. The two textbooks stacked there seemed to mock him. He should be studying. He had one helluva test facing him tomorrow, and he hadn't even begun to prepare. But he didn't want to study; hell, he didn't want to do anything except think about Joanna and how he'd ached to keep touching her.

He looked down at his hands. They shook. A curse singed the air. His insides were a raw mass of nerves, and he couldn't think straight.

From the onset, he'd seen Joanna as an intellect with no practical knowledge or sense of the real world. Why that had rankled him, he hadn't known. Maybe he'd equated her attitude with snobbery.

Nonetheless, he sensed he could get back at her snobbish intellect through his ability to ruffle her composure. That was what had driven him, to see if anything had smoldered underneath, to see what made her fear him one minute and desire him the next.

He'd accomplished his mission. Fire definitely flamed beneath that cool surface. Yet he felt no satisfaction because his mission had backfired. He was the one who was shaking on the inside.

From now on, though, he'd live by his vow and wouldn't think about how she'd looked in that bathing suit—as if she'd been melted and poured into it— or how soft her skin was to the touch, or how sweet it smelled. Least of all, he wouldn't think about how his body had wanted to explode from not having her.

His gut-biting need for her was foolish and had to be controlled. He mustn't let his guard down, must not allow himself to be swept away by his emotions.

"I'm leaving now."

Her soft, husky voice brought him around. Joanna, now dressed, stood slightly inside his office. "Do you have to leave?" he asked.

She stood still, a question in her eyes.

Mike's mind raced. Let it go, for god's sake. She's not for you. She doesn't like men, and she'll rip your heart into tiny pieces. "Wanna go somewhere and get a cup of coffee?"

Eight

Joanna barely kept her mouth from gaping, shock and wariness reflected in her eyes. "Now?"

He hiked a leg on the edge of his desk in a nonchalant manner, but the look in his eyes was anything but nonchalant. Tension, thicker than the morning's fog, fell over the room.

"Well?" The controlled expression on Mike's face did not change.

Joanna's stomach lurched painfully while a tiny voice whispered, *No, don't go. You'll be sorry.* But her curiosity was piqued. Despite his obvious contempt for her intellectual ability, she knew he wasn't immune to her as a woman. She'd seen the fire in his eyes, felt it in his hand when he'd touched her. Oh, God, remembering the feel of those hands sent her pulses skyrocketing again.

She rarely did anything daring, spontaneous; she thought everything through from all angles. She didn't see any reason to change things now. Still . . . there was something about this man.

Mike lunged off the desk, interrupting her racing thoughts. "Obviously the answer is no," he said flatly.

"I'd love some coffee."

Her softly spoken acceptance seemed to jolt him like a live wire. He jerked his head up, then eased into his trademark smile that relaxed the lines around his mouth. Joanna's heart did an involuntary flip-flop.

"Then let's go."

"Where to?"

"This buddy of mine just opened a—" He broke off and stifled an expletive.

"What's wrong?"

"Nothing. It's just that I figured you wouldn't be interested in going to a country-and-western bar."

"Believe me I've been to bars before," she said in a prim tone.

He drew back. "Really?

Damn him. He was making fun of her. "Yes, really."

"So you're game?"

"I'm game."

They left the gym and walked out into the sunshine. Although the time was nearing seven, the sun had lost none of its punch. Joanna paused and reached into her purse for her sunglasses. Once they were in place, she peered at him and asked, "Do you want me to follow you?"

"Nah, I'll bring you back to pick up your car, that is if you don't mind riding in my Jeep."

There it was again, that mocking undertone. He made her out to be a snob. She couldn't help but wonder if that was the way others perceived her—or was it just him.

"No," she said, voicing her irritation, "I don't mind riding in your Jeep."

One black eyebrow rose, and his lips twitched. "Good."

"Your apology's accepted."

His laugh was belly deep as he held the door open for her.

When they pulled into a parking place in front of a whitewashed metal building off F.M. 1960, Joanna threw him an incredulous look.

"Is this it?"

"Yep."

"Why, it's brand-new."

"True, but it's still a place where a lot of rednecks hang out."

"What about you?"

He took the key from the ignition. "I've had my moments."

She smiled tightly. "That's what I thought."

He stared at her with an amused look on his face that she had to fight not to slap off. Finally he climbed out of the vehicle, came around and opened the door for her.

Joanna took a deep breath as she walked beside him. It had taken them thirty minutes to get there.

Throughout the drive, they had spoken very little. But the traffic had been heavy and that had taken most of Mike's concentration. For the most part, she'd kept her mind blank, not wanting to delve into her motives for accompanying him here.

"What do you think?"

Mike's question came after they stepped into the dim interior. She'd been so lost in thought that she hadn't realized he was so close behind her. Shock waves rippled down her back. It was partly due to his warm, minty breath that fanned her neck and cheek. Mostly it was nerves. It took all her effort to keep her footing.

"What do you think?" he repeated.

She blinked. "It's nice."

"Here comes Harry." Mike prodded her forward. "He's the owner and one helluva fellow."

"Mike, my boy—it's good to see you."

The man Mike identified as Harry chuckled as he slapped Mike hard on the shoulder, then cast an inquisitive look in Joanna's direction. To say he was fat would have been an understatement. Yet he carried his weight well despite the fact that he was at least three inches under Mike's height. He had on jeans, plaid shirt, scuffed boots and a Stetson.

"You old misfit, you. How have you been?" Mike asked.

"Why, me and the missus been working our a—" he stopped, glanced at Joanna again, then amended the sentence "—er, rears off to get this club running smoothly."

"Looks like you're on the right road." Mike paused at the same time he turned to Joanna. "Harry Barfield, Joanna Nash."

"Howdy, ma'am. Welcome to Harry's Bar and Grill."

"Thank you." Joanna smiled and returned his handshake.

"Follow me for the best seats in the place."

This time, Mike's hand circled her arm as they followed Harry through a throng of tables, some filled, some empty. Joanna was oblivious to the goings-on around her, even the music that blared from the jukebox. The fact that Mike was touching her again consumed her thoughts.

Joanna only relaxed after they were seated in the rear near a row of windows at a table with a checkered tablecloth. Even then, she avoided his eyes, fearing that he could read the turmoil raging inside her.

"What can I get for you?" Harry asked.

"Coffee for me, please."

"Make that two," Mike said. Then he turned to Joanna. "Do you want something to eat? Harry's specialty is barbecue."

"No, thanks. After that workout, I'm not hungry."

Harry looked shocked. "No food? No beer?"

"Not this afternoon." Mike grinned. "I have another appointment."

"Promise me that you'll bring your lady friend back later."

"I promise." When they were alone, Mike added, "Harry's like a father to me."

"It's obvious you two are close."

"Yeah, old Harry's saved my butt on many occasions. I met him at the gym where I've boxed for years. He's what you call a boxing enthusiast, but he made money in oil, then lost it." Mike smiled. "This club is another indulgent whim."

"It must be nice...to indulge in your whims, I mean."

"Ah, come on, I bet you do that every day." There was a teasing glint in his eye.

"Do you?"

"You damn right I indulge myself. When you grow up in a household of ten siblings, you've earned it."

They were silent as the waitress placed their coffee in front of them, then shuffled off.

"Ten children. There must have been some hard times."

"That's putting it mildly."

Her gaze was held by the turbulence of his eyes. "What about your parents?"

He snorted. "My daddy was downright mean and thought that as long as he provided food and clothing, his responsibility ended."

The ice in his voice could have frozen lava. Yet he had an air of secret woe about him that touched her heart. Besides, she could identify with his pain, having come from a similar type background. Her daddy had simply been too busy for her.

He went on. "So, as soon as I could, I split. Boxing was my first indulgent whim."

She knew her features reflected disapproval.

His lip twisted sardonically. "Have you ever seen a boxing match?"

"Not hardly."

He raised an eyebrow. "Then how do you know you wouldn't like it?"

"Who wants to watch someone get battered and bruised?" She shuddered visibly. "Not me. That's for sure."

He gave her a strange look. "It sounds like you might have experienced some of that bruising first-hand."

Instantly she tensed, but didn't say anything. She wasn't about to let him in on her nasty little secret.

"Maybe you could watch me box sometime?" He grinned as if sensing he had tread into forbidden territory and needed to change the atmosphere. "Better still, you could watch me get punched out."

A sudden twinkle appeared in her eyes. "Now that's not a bad idea. I'll admit there have been times when I'd have liked to punch you out as a payback for torturing me."

He laughed. "Is that a fact, now?"

"That's a definite fact."

"Well, honey, you'll just have to get in line behind a lot of others." He paused, then changed the subject. "What about you? Got any family?"

"My parents are college professors."

"Ever been married?"

"Yes." Her tone was short. "Once."

Something flickered in his eyes. "Don't want to talk about that, huh?

"Right."

"How about work? Will you talk about that?"

She relaxed, feeling once again on solid ground. "There's not a lot to talk about, actually. You'd probably think what I do is dull and boring."

His forehead wrinkled. "You deal with money, don't you?"

"Yes."

"Well, then it isn't boring. The green stuff is what makes the world turn. Only *we* both know your job is far from mundane."

She circled the top of her cup with her index finger. "Oh."

"Don't 'oh' me. I read the papers. I know your ex-boss was caught with his hand in the proverbial cookie jar, using the taxpayers' money for big parties and call girls."

She took a sip of coffee.

"I'm right, aren't I?"

"How did you know that he was my ex-boss?"

"Calvin told me."

"I see." Her voice had an edge to it.

"Is there a problem with that?" he asked, taking a healthy gulp of his coffee.

"Yes. I'd rather not talk about that, either, if you don't mind."

"Ah, hell, don't get all huffy on me." Although his tone was light, his eyes had a steely glint. "Just because your boss was a crooked SOB is no reflection on you."

"Some people don't see it that way."

"I'm not 'some people.' I say you need to lighten up. Okay?"

"And I should do just as you say?"

"Yeah."

She laughed. "Okay."

He watched her closely for a long moment. "You ought to do that more often."

"What?"

"Laugh."

Their eyes met, almost covertly, before they both glanced away.

The coffee suddenly became hard to swallow. "I should?" Joanna asked inanely.

"It looks good on you."

"I've never heard it put quite like that." She recognized the breathless tremor in her voice for what it was, and instantly she was scared. Whoa, slow down, she cautioned silently, reminding herself that this sexual bantering was dangerous. He wasn't the type of man who made commitments. She wasn't the type to give herself without them.

"I have some tickets to the Astros game Saturday night." His strong voice broke into the hush. "You want to go with me?"

A silence fell between them.

Joanna fought off a light-headed feeling and tried to think straight. But she couldn't, not with him looking at her that way. "That sounds like fun."

"Is that a yes?"

"Yes, that's a yes." Her voice was a tight whisper.

His breath came out slowly and soundlessly. "You won't regret it."

Joanna wasn't so sure. For the second time in one day, she found herself saying yes to a man whom she feared would make her wounds start to bleed again.

Nine

The evening was perfect, a star-studded night. Even the cruel South Texas humidity was low, which made the comfort factor extremely pleasant.

Whether the weather was clear or cloudy, hot or cold made little difference as the ball game was played inside, in the Astrodome, considered by many as one of the Wonders of the World. Joanna had only been inside the dome once, and that had been years ago. She'd been impressed with its size and magnificence, but that was all. She couldn't have cared less about the sporting event then, nor did she now.

Yet, here she was at a game. Out of the corner of her eye, she glanced at Mike, who was watching the pregame show with keen interest. She turned her attention there, as well, but she couldn't concentrate on the high school band that paraded around the field, marching in time to a Madonna hit tune. Her mind swarmed with thoughts of how foolish she was.

The instant she'd told Mike she'd go to the game with him, regret had set in. It was one thing to have coffee with him—Lord knows that was innocent enough—but to accept a date was just plain stupid. Here she was, though, sitting beside him, feeling her heart pound every time she looked at him.

He was dressed in jeans, boots and a yellow shirt. Shirt and jeans were stretched taut over his shoulders and thighs, making him seem intimidatingly powerful. He smelled good, too; his cologne aroused her senses with its woodsy aroma.

The entire time she'd berated herself for her behavior, she'd been planning what she was going to wear, almost with the same intensity and excitement as a teenager dressing for her first date. When she'd opened the door and greeted him, she'd known she'd chosen the right outfit. His eyes had lighted and sparked with smoldering desire, taking in her purple silk walking shorts, hot pink blouse, and floral blazer.

"You look great," he'd said.

Joanna had avoided his gaze, but felt color singe her cheeks. "Thanks."

"Are you ready for the big game?" A teasing warmth had further softened his tone.

She'd flushed. "As ready as I'll ever be."

Now, as she waited for the opening play, Joanna looked around, amazed at the number of people in the stadium and their enthusiasm for the sport. The group seated behind her was having a high old time, each person holding a beer and gulping it with a frenzy.

She frowned in distaste, certain that sooner or later she would feel a portion down her back.

"Is something wrong?"

She faced Mike, who was looking at her closely. "Not really. I'm a little concerned about that rowdy crew behind us."

Mike swung around, then turned back to her. "Yeah. They're boozing it up, all right. If they get too rowdy, Security'll toss them out on their ears."

"Good."

"So what do you think?"

"About what?"

He grinned. "Stop playing the innocent."

"I can hardly wait for the first pitch to be thrown."

"Sure."

She smiled. "What did you expect?"

"Do you know anything about baseball?"

"Enough," she said airily.

His eyes were rich with amusement, but he didn't call her bluff. Instead he asked, "Want something to eat or drink?"

She hesitated. "A Coke sounds good."

He stood. "I'll be right back."

While he was gone, Joanna watched and listened to the crowd yell as the players ran onto the field. The starting lineups were then introduced. On the first pitch, Mike eased back into the seat beside her, holding a Coke and can of beer.

"You know this is a do-or-die game for the Astros," he said, handing her the soft drink.

"You know I don't."

"Well, there's always hope," he drawled. "Yep, from here on, every game's crucial if they hope to make the play-offs."

"That probably accounts for the large crowd, huh?"

"Right. When the Astros don't win, the people stay home. Like you," he added, before raising his beer to his lips.

She opened her mouth to reply, only to snap it shut. She couldn't continue mouthing platitudes when she was so conscious of his body next to hers, so close that each time he moved, she felt an electric shock.

She must have made a face because she felt Mike's eyes on her. "Are you okay?"

She didn't dare look at him for fear of what he'd read in her eyes. "I'm fine," she lied. "I just moved a little too quickly, that's all."

"That's a good sign. Shows your muscles are returning to life. That means soon you'll be rid of me." He smiled suddenly, but it didn't reach his eyes.

"And you'll be rid of me," she countered a trifle breathlessly.

Their eyes met, and Joanna felt a total destruction of her senses. Frightened, she was the first to look away.

"Joanna?"

She heard the husky note in his tone and was about to face him again when it happened. One of the men behind her lunged to his feet. His beer bottle tilted and the contents splattered onto Joanna's back.

She cried out. Mike jumped to his feet and whipped around. Joanna followed suit.

"What the hell!" Mike said.

The blond-haired man responsible was oblivious to both of them. His contorted features bore down on the man who stood facing him, so close, they were almost nose to nose.

"Why, you sonofabitch!" the blond yelled.

"You're the sonofabitch!" his cohort retaliated in an even louder voice. "I told you to keep your hands off my wife."

"Why don't you tell your wife to keep her hands off me!"

Foul words spewed from the heavyset man's mouth as he drew back and punched the blond in the face. Blood spurted from his nose.

Mike swore and reached for Joanna, but it was too late. The other men in the party sprang to their feet and began swinging. The women screamed. Pandemonium broke out as all the surrounding spectators got to their feet.

Mike's large body shielded Joanna. "Someone get Security!" he hollered, while stepping into the aisle and pulling Joanna with him. "Come on, let's get the hell out of here."

Trembling, Joanna clung to his hand and followed him up the steps and finally out of the building.

She didn't so much as breathe until she was in his car. But that didn't help. Already she could feel the blood seep from her head, a tightness in her chest, weakness in her limb, and a darkness at the edge of her vision.

"Joanna, talk to me. Are you all right?"

She nodded in the affirmative, but then her slender shoulders began shaking. Tears gathered in her eyes and ran down her cheeks.

"Oh, God, don't," Mike muttered, reaching for her.

Joanna threw up her hands, then cowed against the door. "No! Don't touch me."

He drew back as if she'd slapped him. "What the hell . . . ?"

"They just can't use their heads," she whispered tightly.

"What are you talking about? You're not making sense."

"I am, too, making sense," she lashed out. "You're just not listening."

Mike's breath came out in an audible sigh. "Maybe that's because I don't understand."

"Men who settle things with their fists are no better than animals." Joanna shivered in distaste. "And that's a crying shame."

"Ah, now I get it." Mike's tone was as cold and flat as his eyes. "You're including me in that assessment, right?"

"I didn't say that."

"You didn't have to."

Joanna didn't respond.

"I saw the way you looked when I told you I boxed, but at the time I didn't think much about it. Now, I know what you were thinking, that I use my fists in the same way."

She flinched visibly, but didn't deny it.

"Joanna, what's this all about, really?"

"I don't know what you're taking about," she said, hysteria bubbling close to the surface.

"Yes, you do. Did your ex-husband hurt you?"

The unexpected softening of his tone was almost Joanna's undoing. Tears splashed onto her blouse.

"You might as well tell me. We're not budging till you do."

Joanna dug in her purse and pulled out a tissue. "There's not much to tell," she said tonelessly. "My... husband, Andy, had a violent temper. When he didn't get his way, he'd go berserk."

"Did he ever hit you?"

"Once."

"The bastard!"

Her heart felt wintry and gray. "I left him immediately, but I've never forgotten the pain, and when someone raises a fist—" She broke off, unable to go on.

For the longest time they sat cloaked in the silence.

Mike stared at her delicate profile and felt a chill move over his skin.

"I would never hurt you," he said thickly. "I want you to know that."

She licked her lips. "I'm sorry I panicked. I didn't mean to."

"You were entitled."

Even though Mike knew he couldn't, the ache to haul her into his arms, to bury his face in the soft fragrance of her neck and simply hold her until that stark, haunted look left her eyes intensified with each second that passed.

Then he'd like to hunt down the bastard who had hurt her and give him the thrashing of his life. But that wasn't the answer and he knew it. Besides, the talk of violence would drive her farther away, and he didn't want that...or did he? He'd never been more confused in his life. He just knew that continuing to see this woman beside him would be his downfall.

"It's time I took you home," he said suddenly and without emotion.

They didn't say anything until Mike steered his vehicle into her driveway.

"You want to come in?" she asked, facing him.

"Do you want me to?"

Silence.

"Only if you want to."

The look in her eyes and the husky note in her voice heated Mike's blood. She sounded like a woman who wanted, *needed* to be touched. Yet her hand was on the door handle as if poised for flight if he made such a move. It had been that way from the start—one mixed signal after another, which, he knew, had kept him interested.

Not that he needed any help on that score. He'd taken one look at her and wanted her, despite the fact that he'd denied it at every turn. He would have already made his move had she not been so skittish. Now, though, he knew the reason behind her action. Still, it didn't stop him from aching to show her how it could be between a man and woman with mutual desires. And she was looking at him as though she wanted him.

He stared at her for a long moment while the air between them crackled with electricity. He swallowed another curse before yanking open the door and getting out.

"Are you sure you wouldn't rather have a beer?" Joanna asked, having returned to the living room carrying a tray filled with two cups of coffee and cookies.

"No, coffee's fine."

Joanna set the tray on the table in front of the couch then sat down herself, careful to place a safe distance between them. For a moment neither spoke, lost in their own thoughts.

In light of what had just taken place, Joanna was questioning her judgment in asking him in. But she hadn't wanted to be alone, not just yet. And she owed him an apology. She'd been wrong to compare Mike with her ex-husband. Even if he was like him, it was none of her business. Mike's presence in her life was only temporary. After tonight, she wouldn't see him again outside the club.

"I like your place," Mike said, his gaze wandering around the room.

She smiled, feeling less tense inside. "Thanks. I thought long and hard before I decided to settle on a house. But now I'm glad I did."

Her gaze tracked his, seeing her home through his eyes. She'd been told that her house looked like a page from *House Beautiful*. At one end of the living room, a beautiful brick fireplace served as the focal point. At the other end, a state-of-the art entertainment center held all the latest high-tech equipment. Behind the sofa were a piano, plants, a table bearing knickknacks and photographs.

"I didn't think I could handle apartment life any longer," Joanna finally said.

"I know what you mean." Mike rested an ankle across his knee. "Car doors slam at all hours of the day and night, there's constant movement."

"Exactly. I just didn't want to live like that anymore."

"Look, I'm sorry about tonight."

His sudden change of subject caught her momentarily off guard. "Forget it."

"I can't."

"I was wrong," she said haltingly. "I should never have lumped you—"

"I hope that SOB pays for what he did to you."

"He won't." Her tone was bitter. Then she switched the subject. "How much longer do you think it'll be before I'm one hundred percent fit?"

The light flared in his eyes. "You just can't wait to dump my services, can you?"

She flushed and avoided his gaze. "It's...not that."

"Yes, it is," he teased. "Well, if it's any consolation, you're not the only one who would like to tar and feather me."

"I was thinking of something quicker, but just as deadly."

"Oh, and what would that be?"

"A hit man."

They looked at each other, then erupted into laughter, only to have the laughter suddenly cease. The moment turned critical.

"Joanna," Mike whispered achingly.

Ten

Joanna's bewildered eyes widened as his face inched nearer. Panic took over, and a moan escaped her. She ached desperately to shut her eyes, to ignore the light-headedness that made the room spin, to pretend that this moment wasn't happening. But the next moment his hand circled the back of her neck and his mouth came down on hers, stopping another moan.

His lips were tentative at first. But suddenly, as if the quivering softness of hers knocked his restraints aside, the kiss deepened. Tongues touched, then tangled hungrily, greedily. Warm breaths were exchanged. His hot, moist lips trailed across her cheek and neck, taking delicate bites. His saliva bathed her.

A groan broke from him; then just as quickly as the kiss had begun, it ended. He pulled away, his breath coming in short, gasping spurts.

They stared at each other...

It was Mike who broke the heavy silence. "Look, Joanna, I—"

"Please, don't say anything," she said thickly. "Just go."

He stared at her again, long and hard, a muscle ticking in his jaw. Following a muttered curse, he rose and stamped to the door.

Joanna, her body trembling out of control, sank farther into the sofa.

"Ms. Nash, Detective Mason."

"Good morning," Joanna said, curbing the uneasiness that skidded through her. She just wished the police would bow out of her life. To date, they'd still found nothing concrete to confirm their suspicions about the hit-and-run. Yet they held on to those suspicions tenaciously, continuing to give her around-the-clock protection.

"I'm just checking in to make sure you haven't had any strange phone calls or had anything out of the ordinary happen that I should know about."

Joanna eased back in the chair at her desk and watched a bird outside the window perch on an electric line and flap his wings. "Not a thing, but if it had, you'd be the first to know."

"I'm counting on it."

"So, don't you think you can pull your man off the case now?"

"Not just yet."

Joanna swallowed her sigh. "I'll do whatever you think best."

Detective Mason chuckled, confirming that he heard the note of agitation in her voice. "I'll be in touch. Have a good day."

"You, too."

Joanna placed the receiver back in the cradle, walked to the tiny coffee bar in the corner and poured herself a cup of coffee. While sipping on the hot liquid, her gaze wandered back to her desk. The folder that was labeled FDIC claimed her attention. Not only did she have that project awaiting her attention, but there were several others.

Unfortunately, she couldn't concentrate on anything. It was as if Mike had hot-wired both her mind and body. She blamed him entirely. No, that wasn't fair; *she* was to blame.

Even now the thought of that deep, sucking kiss they had exchanged made her cringe. How could she have lost control so easily? She had always prided herself on being a cautious, sensible person who, with rational thinking, could overcome anything. Yet, she hadn't been able to overcome her fascination with Mike or the tactics he used against her.

Somehow she had to end this madness between them. Mike was more than a threat to her peace of mind; he was a threat to her future. There were so many reasons why a relationship with him wouldn't work. Her mind cataloged them immediately. He came on too strong. She was into mind games; he was into body games. He was much too physical, too passionate for her. She didn't want to feel that much, to ache for a man.

She was a tad uptight, choosing to keep her emotions low-key. She admitted that. But she wouldn't apologize for feeling that way, especially after what she'd suffered at the hands of her ex-husband.

As far as Mike was concerned, he apparently had no such reservations. He didn't know the first thing about controlling his emotions. In fact, he was far too free with his words and his hands. Both he used with skill—especially his hands. He had only to touch her and her insides turned to putty. But, dear Lord, she didn't want or need this turbulence in her life, this continued yanking at her heartstrings.

If and when she decided to enter into another relationship, she wanted a man who offered calm stability, who thought and felt as she did. Mike simply was not that man. He was a ladies' man, pure and simple, with no intention of settling down to a home and family. Falling in love he seemed to do well. It was staying in love that presented the problem.

From now on, she had to be true to herself and her values. She would *not* see Mike outside the club. Period.

Calvin tapped on the door. She looked up with a start.

"Are you about ready to go?" he asked.

Thankful for the timely interruption, Joanna smiled, then reached for the folder in front of her. "I'm ready."

Calvin grimaced. "Let's just hope the bank examiners are in a good mood. Maybe they ate their Wheaties this morning."

"I'm not worried," Joanna said with an air of confidence, patting her briefcase. "Everything's documented."

She had been preparing for this meeting for days. Three men from the FDIC were there to scrutinize several of their large transactions. While the meeting would be tough, Joanna felt the bank had the ammunition needed to win.

"By the way, how's the exercising going?" Calvin asked as they walked out of her office.

Joanna wrinkled her nose. "Don't ask."

Calvin chuckled. "That bad, huh? Well, just keep in mind it won't last forever."

"Please, keep reminding me of that."

When they reached the conference room door, Calvin paused and glanced down at his watch. "They're waiting inside, I'm sure."

"That's fine. I'll welcome a fight, if that's to be." And she would. Anything was preferable to thoughts of Mike.

She smiled and squared her shoulders. "Let's go."

Where the hell was she?

An icy feeling surrounded Mike's heart. Maybe she decided she wasn't coming back. He looked at his watch for the umpteenth time and saw that only a minute had passed since he'd looked at it last.

"Damn," he muttered, walking to the window and staring outside into the rain. What a miserable day. The Houston marathon loomed near, and he wanted to get in shape. He'd started to run in the rain, but when thunder cracked and lightning flashed, he'd gone to class early instead.

He'd arrived back at the club around noon, and the rain hadn't let up, nor had his bad mood. Both had steadily progressed from bad to worse. He'd needed that run. He'd counted on it curing his pounding head.

He wanted Joanna so badly that it had made him physically ill. Why the hell had he kissed her? He'd asked himself that a million times since they'd had coffee. He'd had no answer then, nor did he now.

Joanna was not the type of woman he should mess around with. She wouldn't tolerate one-night stands; that was all he wanted. So how did he get her out of his system? His mood brightened. Maybe once he took her, his interest in her would die a natural death.

Fat chance, McCoy.

He wiped the gathering sweat from his face, peered at his watch again, then muttered, "To hell with it."

His gaze went to the phone. He'd call and see what was going on, he decided, guilt rising like bile up the back of his throat. If he'd kept his hands off her, her absence wouldn't be a problem. This wouldn't be happening. He'd never lost a client due to unprofessionalism. He feared, however, Joanna might be the first.

What if she carried through with her earlier threat to fire him? He damn well wouldn't let her. She'd made progress, all right, but she wasn't one hundred percent fit by any means. She still needed his help.

After getting her phone number from her folder, Mike lifted the receiver and punched out her number. He listened as it rang to no avail. After he hung up, he plopped down in his chair. He'd wait. Maybe she'd show up.

From a distance he saw that the house was dark. His heart sank. She wasn't home. Instead of turning around, Mike nosed the Jeep farther down the lamplighted street until he was directly in front of her house.

Her car was parked in the driveway. He pulled his vehicle close to the curb and stared at the dark house.

Was he a fool for coming here? Probably, but he'd had no other choice. She hadn't shown up. He'd screwed up when he kissed her. He had to make amends. So, he'd decided, hell, he'd just go to her house and apologize, even if it was ten o'clock.

The decision hadn't come easily. He'd stewed and paced until he'd about worn a hole in his office carpet. Then he'd had several clients he'd had to take care of. Now was the first chance he'd had to get away from the club. He'd considered calling her again, but what he had to say shouldn't be said over the phone.

Ignoring the tight band around his chest, Mike yanked open the door and got out. His steps up the walk were fast and deliberate. He leaned on the doorbell. No response.

The decision to tramp around back seemed logical; since her car was in the drive, it stood to reason that she was home. Clinging to that rationalization, he walked onto the deck and up to the French doors. Through the sheer curtains he saw a dim light shining from the kitchen, which allowed him to see inside.

No sight of Joanna.

He lifted his hand to knock when a harsh voice growled in his ear, "Don't move."

He moved.

"I said, don't move."

It was then that he felt the cold barrel of a gun in his ribs.

Eleven

Joanna sat straight up in bed and for a moment, the only sound she heard was the loud pounding in her chest. What had awakened her so suddenly? Had she been having a nightmare?

Then she heard the—voices, loud voices. That commotion was what had roused her from a deep sleep. Her heart thudded with fear. Without stopping to answer the questions swirling inside her head, she tossed back the afghan, jumped up and hurried out of the bedroom.

She realized the voices were coming from the deck. The full moon dazzled the room in light. She heard the clock chime ten-thirty. But the time barely registered as she peered through the sheers on the French doors where she saw the silhouettes of three men. She recognized the voices of the two men exchanging terse words.

Expelling her breath sharply, Joanna flipped the lock and opened one side of the door. Silence fell immediately as all eyes focused on her.

She had eyes for only one—Mike. They darted gazes at each other like enemies sizing up each other.

He was the first to glance away, his lips stretched in a rigid line. Standing next to him was the plainclothesman, Jeff Neely. Mike and Jeff had been the ones talking. She didn't know the third man, a uniformed officer.

"What's going on here?" she demanded, grinding her teeth together.

Jeff Neely pawed at the wood on the deck with the toe of his boot, then raised his head. "Sorry for all the commotion, ma'am, but we caught this man sneaking—"

"Oh, for god's sake," Mike interrupted, "I wasn't sneaking."

Jeff ignored him and went on. "When I confronted him, he became belligerent."

Mike grunted. "Only after you shoved a gun in my ribs."

Joanna felt as if the wind had been knocked out of her. "What?"

"You heard me," Mike said. "And I don't take too kindly to being threatened, especially when I haven't done anything."

"We didn't know that, Mr. McCoy," Neely said patiently. "It's my... our job to protect Ms. Nash."

"Pray tell from what?" Mike looked at Joanna. "What's he talking about?"

Before she could answer, Neely jumped in again. "He says he's a friend of yours." His gaze switched from Mike to Joanna. "Is that right?"

She slanted a look in Mike's direction. Judging from the scowl on his face and the continued tightness around his mouth, he could easily have bitten a tenpenny nail in two.

"Yes, that's right." Her words came out in a rush.

"Well, we had to be sure." Neely faced his companion. "By the way, Ms. Nash, this is Officer Browning, who will be replacing me on the watch."

"Do you think that's absolutely necessary?" Joanna asked, not bothering to keep the exasperation out of her tone.

"I'm just following Detective Mason's order, ma'am."

"Then I'll talk to the detective myself," she said tersely.

Neely nodded. "Fine, ma'am."

A silence followed.

"We'll be going now," Neely announced into the awkward silence.

"Thank you," Joanna forced herself to say.

Neely nodded again, then, flashing Mike another look, he motioned for his partner to follow him. Both Joanna and Mike stood in silence as the officers disappeared around the side of the house into the darkness.

Joanna forced her attention back on Mike. Her gaze wandered from his jogging shoes, to his bare legs covered in dark hair, to his gym shorts, up to the striped T-shirt and over the strong chin. He needed a shave. His eyes were cold and angry.

She swallowed against the dryness in her throat. "They didn't hurt you, did they?"

"Not hardly."

Her cheeks reddened with a rush of blood. "That's a relief."

"Look, do you mind if we continue this conversation inside?"

"Uh, sorry." Joanna turned and walked across the threshold. He followed, then closed the door behind him.

They paused midway into the room, saying nothing. Dread seeped through Joanna as Mike suddenly appeared big, angry and intimidating.

"What the hell's going on here?" His tone was low, urgent.

She fought for the right words. "There...there's a plainclothesman watching my house."

"Tell me something I don't know."

"I'm sorry he mistook you for—"

"Who? Who did he mistake me for?"

She took a deep breath and let it out. "I'm trying to tell you, but you won't let me. Not that I owe you an explanation, that is," she added defiantly.

"That's true, but—"

"What were you doing at my back door?"

Her unexpected questioning of him seemed to catch him off guard for a moment. She watched as the muscles bunched in his cheeks.

"I came to find out why you didn't show up for the session."

"I see."

"So why didn't you?"

Had his tone thickened or was it her imagination playing tricks on her? "I had an exhausting day at work, so I told myself I'd rest for a few minutes, then go to the club." She paused, avoiding his smoldering gaze. "But I fell asleep and didn't wake up until I heard the noise."

Only part of what she said was true. She'd been exhausted all right, but she'd decided to sever the business relationship with Mike and find another trainer. The kiss had unnerved her so much that her work had suffered. She hadn't been able to concentrate on anything except her response to him. The thought of seeing him again had been untenable.

"It's your turn to come clean," he prodded, his eyelids at half-mast.

"Look, you're making too big a deal of this."

"Let me be the judge of that." His tone plunged five degrees. "Anyhow, when someone jams a gun in your ribs, I think that's a pretty big deal."

"You're right, it is."

"I'm waiting."

Still she hesitated.

"Dammit, Joanna!"

"Oh, all right," she said, and told him about her ex-boss and the upcoming trial with herself as a key witness.

When she finished, his face turned noticeably pale, and his eyes reminded her of chips of dark ice. "So they think the hit-and-run is related?"

"Uh-huh."

"Do you?"

"No. I've told Detective Mason that."

"Who's he?"

"The officer in charge."

"Hell, Joanna, if they've got you under police surveillance, they must have reason to believe you're in some kind of danger. Otherwise they wouldn't waste manpower."

"They're just making a mountain out of a molehill."

He moved suddenly and before she knew it, he towered over her, his legs slightly spread, his features pinched in a fierce frown. "Are you nuts?"

"Don't you dare talk to me like that!"

He jammed his hands in his pocket as if fighting his frustration. When he spoke again, his tone was softer, but the note of agony was still there. "Don't you understand, if anything happened to you—"

Joanna sucked in her breath and battled the urge to stop breathing completely.

"God, Joanna, don't look at me like that." His voice sounded hoarse, unrecognizable.

The connective force between them was so strong it seemed tangible.

Joanna backed up, suddenly conscious that she was naked under her robe. Wordlessly, their eyes remained locked, that torrid kiss uppermost in their minds.

Determined to break the spell and clear her head, Joanna lifted her arm to rub her temple. Her hand stopped in midair when his indrawn breath turned into a gasp, followed by the broken words, "What are you trying to do to me?"

It was then that she realized what had happened. Her sudden movement had dislodged her robe so that a portion of her breast was exposed.

She looked down, then back, dragging air into her burning lungs. "I..." she began, wanting to move, to run, to hide, but she couldn't.

The hot longing in his eyes, in his voice, held her captive. She could only stand there and watch helplessly as he stepped even closer.

Without moving his eyes from her, he reached out and touched her face.

"Mike," she whispered, her breath coming in short rasps.

She was beautiful, he thought, her breast still exposed to his gaze. He knew now what Adam must have felt. He, too, had glimpsed the forbidden. He could feel his heart; it drummed in his chest, while fire scorched his veins.

The moonlight dappled across her face and turned her eyes into dark, unclouded pools. She returned his stare, her focus seeming to soak up his features, slowly, methodically, as if committing each detail to memory.

He continued to caress her. "Your skin...it feels like velvet," he said in a strangled tone.

Her eyes encouraged him to keep touching her. He needed no second invitation. The pad of a thumb gently outlined her full lower lip.

She closed her eyes and began shaking.

The feel of those trembling lips sent pleasure ribboning through him bringing him to an explosive erection. Guttural sounds came from him as he reached out slowly and untied the sash around her waist, then slipped the robe from her shoulders.

Long-limbed, high-hipped, she redefined the word *perfection.* And her breasts—they were small but firm with petite nipples, not much larger than his own.

The light washed over them, taunting him with their rose-hued beauty. Her breath rippled and drew his attention to her flat stomach.

"You're in the dark," she whispered, clutching at him. Her fingertips sank into the solidity of his muscles. He crushed her against him and pulled her cheek onto his chest. Bonded together, they inched their way to the plush rug splayed across the carpet.

Words weren't necessary. Only the ecstasy of the unplanned, unprepared moment, when flesh met flesh, was all that mattered. Breaking away, Mike peeled his clothes from his body, and once again pulled her nakedness against his hardness.

He kissed her sensual lips, partly opened, then moved his mouth along her cheek, the side of her neck, the dip in her collarbone, stopping only when he reached the creamy curve of her breasts. He cupped them, drew a nipple between two fingers and toyed with it.

Joanna's chest heaved visibly, and she moaned just as he lowered his lips to close over that same nipple, teasing it with his tongue, then gently sucking on it. He returned to her mouth and sank his lips onto hers once again, devouring their sweetness.

"Oh, Mike," she whispered, running her hands over his shoulders, neck, back, down to the taut mounds of his buttocks.

His heartbeat faltered, and he felt feverish. "Yes, oh, yes," Mike said, moving a finger to the juncture of her thighs and placing pressure there.

Her eyelashes fluttered against his bare shoulder. She moaned, moving her head from side to side. Unrecognizable sounds emanated from her, sounds of lust. Her nails sank deep into his buttocks.

Pleasure throbbed inside him. He never wanted this moment to end. He thought only of pleasing her, something foreign to him. For so long, from one relationship to another, he hadn't particularly concerned himself with his mate's pleasure, only his own. Now, he not only cared, but he was obsessed that Joanna come away satisfied, knowing that only through her fulfillment would he reach his own.

She whimpered in a climax. Fingers of pleasure raced into his groin, arousing him. He moved on top of her, and without hesitation her legs parted. His hot flesh slid into her, and she whimpered again, receiving him.

His thrusts were slow and easy at first, while his lips drew on a nipple. Her legs curled around him, her tongue mated with his savagely. Yet her touch to his flesh was so exquisite that he felt his muscles jump.

Time lost its meaning. Desire clogged his throat, making speech impossible. Only moans, gasps and cries filled the room. Soon his patience came to an end. He stroked deeper, longer, faster. She moved with him, withering, encouraging his sweet assault on her body.

Then finally it came—that magic relief. Their coupling intensified.

"Joanna, Joanna..."

Her name was spoken through punctuated gasps as the anticipatory spasms reached a crescendo. Finally he spilled his seed from his body into hers.

Twelve

They lay naked and spent; the bed was a mess. The bottom sheet had worked loose; pillows were strewn on the bed and floor. They couldn't have cared less, so intent were they on gazing at each other out of passion and gratitude. Soon, though, exhaustion forced their eyes to drift shut and oblivion laced with extreme satisfaction claimed them.

Joanna was the first to awaken. When her eyes opened, she was confused. She twisted her head slightly and saw him. Her breath caught in her throat as she took in the peaceful expression on Mike's face. She watched him for several moments, her thoughts so jumbled she couldn't begin to sort them out.

Then it all came back to her. The torrid lovemaking on the rug in front of the fireplace, followed by their flight into the bedroom where they continued the sweet, savage devouring of each other's bodies.

She turned her gaze to the clock on the bedside table. It said six, barely daylight. Work! She gave a start. She needn't worry; she had plenty of time to get to work.

Her heart settled, and she faced Mike again, quelling the urge to run her hands over the beard that covered his strong jaw. The night in his arms had gone far beyond even her wildest imagination. Mike made her feel as she'd never felt before. But what did that mean? Had she fallen in love? Her stomach rolled into a ball. No. Her attraction to him was sexual—nothing more, nothing less. Love didn't enter into it. Having decided that, she felt better.

"Hi."

Mike's husky voice jerked her back to reality. Suddenly shy, she avoided his direct gaze. "Good morning," she whispered.

The room fell quiet again.

"Are you sorry?"

She looked back at him. "No. Are you?"

"How can you ask that?"

She lowered her eyes while her face flamed. She suddenly remembered the things he'd done to her body, the things she'd done to him.

"Come here."

The husky edge to his tone sent chills racing up her spine. She scooted closer and rested her head in the crook of his arm. They lay quietly for a minute, each lost in their own turbulent thoughts.

"What happens now?"

"What do you mean?" she asked, but she knew. They had not planned for last night. Now that it had happened, they had to face it.

"Will you continue to see me? Outside the club?"

Joanna picked up on the uncertainty in his voice and ached to reassure him. But she couldn't. "Do you think that's wise?"

"No, but I don't give a damn."

She smiled. "Me, either."

His hand cupped an exposed breast. "From the first moment I saw you, I knew you were trouble." He chuckled. "Actually, I thought you were one cold bitch."

She tweaked the hair on his chest.

"Ouch!"

"Serves you right for thinking such bad things about me."

"Boy, was I ever wrong." He lowered his voice to a husky whisper. "I found that you're tight and hot inside and—" His voice shook, then faded.

The color in Joanna's face deepened. "Oh, Mike."

They were both silent for a long time.

"I hate to ask this, but I have to know."

"What?"

"You're not on the Pill, are you?"

"No." Ignoring his shuddering sigh, she went on, "But I think I'm safe. It's not the time of the month for me." She prayed what she said was true, that she hadn't miscalculated.

"That's good. I can't tell you the last time I made love without a condom, but I wanted you so badly, I threw caution to the bloody wind."

"I know," she said in a thin voice.

"Was it this way with your...ex? Was it this...good?"

She sucked in her breath. "Never. He didn't care if I was satisfied or not."

"Then he's a bigger damn fool than I thought."

"He's worse than that."

"Look, I didn't mean to resurrect bad memories. God knows, we all have things better left buried."

"It's all right. I don't mind you knowing."

He pulled her closer. "I want to know everything else there is to know about you."

"I had a baby."

The sadly spoken words fell heavy into the silence.

He raised up, propped his hand on his head and peered down into her upturned face. "A child? You had a child?"

"She was the love of my life." A sob tore at Joanna's throat. "I was devastated when she died."

His heart, next to hers, pounded like a jackhammer. "Died. God, I can't imagine..."

"No, no one can until they experience it."

"You want another child, don't you?"

Warning bells went off inside her head, but she ignored them. "Yes, very much."

She felt him stiffen, and she knew instantly that she should have paid heed to those warnings. "You don't want children, though, do you?"

"No," he said flatly, "I don't."

She distanced herself from him suddenly and shifted her gaze. End it now, she told herself. She didn't need the pain and tears that would surely follow. Only how could she just walk away when she'd just gotten a glimpse of paradise in his arms? She couldn't. It was just that simple and just that complicated.

As if he read her mind, Mike reached for her. "You know I can't let you go."

"It'll never work."

"How do you know?"

"I just do and so do you."

"Because you want kids and I don't?" he asked.

"There's more to it than that, although that's part of it."

He leaned down and tongued her nipple, then sucked it.

She groaned as sparks of heat settled between her thighs. "You're not playing fair."

"I'll play anyway I can to keep you."

"Mike...I—"

His lips cut her off in a soul-searching kiss.

"Let's don't worry about the future," he pleaded, pulling his mouth from hers. "Let's just take one day at a time."

She nodded, her throat too full to speak.

The next two months passed in a blur. As Mike suggested, they took one day at a time and saw each other away from the club as much as they could.

Joanna knew she was thinking with her heart instead of her head, but she couldn't help it. No matter how much she preached to herself that Mike was no good for her, that they were too different to sustain a permanent relationship, she couldn't stop seeing him.

He made her crazy with desire. He made her laugh. He made her angry. But never did he bore her. Her life had gone from mundane to exhilarating.

The only dark spot during this time was her physical inability. She wasn't progressing the way Mike thought she should, despite the increased workout sessions. Then, catching Kim's stomach virus didn't help. Not only did she throw up, but she was listless and irritable, as well. Finally, at Mike's insistence, she went to the doctor, expecting him to give her a fistful of pills and a sermon on how to take better care of herself.

Instead, the doctor walked into the examination room and said, "Ms. Nash, it's not the flu that's continuing to drag you down."

"Oh?"

He smiled. "You're pregnant."

That had been yesterday, and she was still reeling from the shock. She'd been sincere when she'd told Mike she thought she was safe after their first and only time to make love unprotected.

Now, as she walked around her house in a stupor, she kept asking herself what she was going to do. Deep down, the answer was clear. She'd keep the baby, of course. Granted, she was much too old to have made such a costly error in judgment. But since she had, she'd live with her mistake, as she'd lived with many others. No matter what anyone said, she wouldn't knowingly end the pregnancy.

Her hand went automatically to her queasy stomach as she made her way into the kitchen. She'd been home from work only an hour, and today was her off day at the gym. Anyway, Mike was out of town, which couldn't have happened at a better time.

Just as she was adding fresh water to the pot to make coffee, the back door rattled. "Who's there?" she asked.

"Kim."

Kim had been out of town for three days. Joanna hadn't expected her back so soon, but she was always glad to see her, especially this evening.

"I'm glad you're back," Joanna said, opening the door and giving her friend a hug.

"Me, too."

"Did you have a good trip?"

"Same ole' same ole'."

Joanna shut the door and followed Kim into the kitchen where the coffeepot gurgled, filling the air with its rich odor.

Kim plopped down into a chair. "Whew, I'm bushed."

"It's the flu still working on you."

"Nah," Kim said. "It's the job."

Joanna didn't respond. She felt Kim's eyes bore into her back as she filled two cups with coffee. "What's up? You sound down. You're not still sick, are you?"

"Not really." Joanna turned around, her lips curved downward.

"What's that supposed to mean?"

Joanna released a quivering sigh. "Oh, Kim, I think I'm pregnant."

Kim's mouth fell open, then she closed it abruptly while her eyes widened. "You think or you know?"

"I know." Tears stood at the corners of her eyes. "Go ahead, say what you're thinking, that I'm a fool."

Kim recovered quickly. "I'm not about to pass judgment."

"You'd...think I'd have better sense—" Joanna's voice broke, and she couldn't go on.

"Hey," Kim said, jumping up and closing the distance between them. She placed an arm around Joanna's shoulders. "Are you positive? I mean, you've had that infection. Could that—?"

Joanna shook her head, cutting Kim off. "I went to the doctor, and he told me. But still I didn't believe him, so I bought one of those pregnancy test kits. It tested glaringly positive."

"Whoa," Kim said, expelling her breath loudly.

Joanna dashed a tear from her eyes.

"What are you going to do?"

"Keep it, of course."

"Have you told Mike?"

"Not yet."

"Do you love him?"

"Yes."

"So you're not sorry, then?"

Joanna's wan features brightened. "I should be, I know, but I'm not." She paused, her face losing its animation. "But I didn't not take precautions on purpose. It...it just happened."

Kim hugged her again, then moved away. "There's a lot I could say, a lot of concerns I have, but I'm not going to say them. What I am going to say is that you have my support, whatever you decide."

"Thanks, Kim," Joanna said with a watery smile. "I'm going to need it. Not only do I have to face Mike but my parents, as well."

"I know, and that's going to be tough, especially the latter." Kim eased back down at the table. "When . . . are you going to tell Mike?"

"As soon as he gets back. Probably tomorrow night. We're supposed to go out."

Kim's smile fell short of a real one. "It's going to be all right. You wait and see."

"I pray you're right."

Dressed in a lightweight terry jumpsuit, Joanna met Mike at the door. "Hi," she said.

"Hi, yourself." His voice sounded rusty as he leaned and kissed her fully on the lips. "Running late, huh?"

Joanna motioned him inside, then shut the door. She didn't respond until they reached the living room. "Do you mind if we didn't go dancing?"

They had planned to go to Al's Place, a country-and-western dive, to hear a college buddy of Mike's perform. But after she'd visited the doctor and had her suspicions confirmed, dancing was the last thing she wanted to do.

He lifted one eyebrow, then grinned. "My, but this sounds serious." His tone teased. "But then you're always serious, aren't you, honey?"

His attempt to bring an answering smile to Joanna's lips failed. "What I have to tell you is serious."

His features sobered. "What's wrong? Are you sick again?"

"N-no, not r-really," she stammered, concentrating on the painting on the wall.

"What's that supposed to mean?"

"Let's sit down," she said quickly.

He watched her carefully, then shrugged. "Whatever you say."

Joanna faced him on the couch. Her palms were wet; her heart was lodged in her throat. She opened her mouth, then closed it.

"Hey, what's going on?" Mike reached for her hand, raised it to his lips and nibbled on one finger, then another.

"Don't," she said shakily, withdrawing her hand. "That tickles."

"Ah, a smile. I thought for a minute that frown was frozen permanently on your face."

She forced another smile, but it didn't last, either. An internal shudder racked her. "I...we have to talk."

"They've found the bastard who ran you down?"

Joanna blinked. "What?"

Mike repeated what he'd just said.

"No. In fact I haven't heard from Mason in several days."

"Well, that goon is still hanging around, although I can't say I'm not relieved."

Joanna was quiet.

"I'm listening, so spit it out."

She peered at him through tear-washed eyes. "I'm...going to have a baby, Mike. Your baby."

Thirteen

His jaw fell slack, then turned rigid. When the silence took on an ominous ring, he coughed. Joanna heard the breath rattle in his throat. Several seconds passed before he said anything.

"Say that again."

The level of his voice did not change, but the cutting edge made Joanna wince. She gripped the sofa's padded arm. "There's no need. You heard me."

His mouth twisted. "Are you sure?"

"Yes, I'm sure. The doctor confirmed it."

He swore under his breath.

Joanna crossed her arms over her chest and hugged herself, feeling cold and brittle. If she made one sudden move, she feared she would crumble into tiny pieces.

"You're furious, aren't you?" she asked, that coldness seeping into the marrow of her bones.

He gave a curt jerk of his head. "I'm not happy."

His words drew blood as only a jagged blade could do. Dear Lord, her worst fears had come to pass. She'd feared his reaction, yet she had hoped he'd be pleased—despite his opposition to children and despite the fact that they didn't love each other. Only, she did love *him*.

Despair replaced the coldness circling her heart. How on earth had she lost control of her life?

"How do *you* feel?" he asked, attacking his forehead with his fingers as if to stop the uproar behind it. Still, she could see the pulse beating hard in his temple.

The ache inside her oozed a little more. "It was a stupid thing to have let happen." Her voice wavered. "But I can't say I'm unhappy."

"Well, you should be," he said through gritted teeth.

"Look, you don't have to worry." She paused until she regained control her voice. "I'll take full responsibility for what has happened."

"That's not the point."

She bit back the hot words she wanted to say. "What is the point, then?"

"Your health, for god's sake!"

Joanna shook her head in tight angry movements. "My health is fine."

He swore again, then sat on the couch and reached out his arm toward her.

She dodged that action and sank deeper into the cushions. "Don't you dare touch me."

A hush fell. The seconds ticked by. Neither spoke. Joanna tried to ignore the loud buzzing in her ears, but when the room began to spin, she couldn't. She gave in and closed her eyes.

"Joanna," he pleaded in a stricken voice.

She opened her eyes and without looking at him scrambled to her feet, walked to the window and stared out.

"You're making me the bad guy here, and I'm not."

She whirled, her eyes on fire. "How do you figure that? You're mad as hell about the baby."

"No, I'm not mad as hell about the baby. I'm concerned about *you.*"

"Sure."

The air wheezed out of his lungs. "Your body is in no shape to carry a child."

"That's your opinion."

"That's right, it is. But I'm as qualified as anyone to make that judgment."

"It's just guilt gnawing at you."

The anguish in her voice seemed to cut him deeply; he winced. "I won't deny that. I should be strung up by my boots for not taking precautions, only—" He broke off abruptly and turned away. "Hell, we both know why we didn't use anything."

"We...I can't worry about that now." The anger in her eyes merged with stinging tears. "I have to think about the future...about the baby."

"Joanna," he said again, stepping closer to her.

She held out her hand and halted him. "Don't say anything else, please. You've made your position clear.

And, as I said a while ago, you don't have to be concerned.''

"Dammit, you're purposely missing the point."

"No, I'm not. You made it plain from the start that you didn't want any responsibility or commitments. So, I'm not holding you down."

"Exactly what are you saying?" he asked into the sudden quietness.

A single sob tore through her lips, while a tear dislodged and trickled down her cheek. "You know."

"I want to hear you say it." His voice shook.

She jutted her chin. "All right. I don't want or need you in my life." Pain crawled through her words. "You're absolved from all obligations."

He flinched, as if she'd literally dealt him a low blow. And when he spoke, his tone was harsh. "You've misconstrued my feelings and my words. But I can see I'm wasting my time arguing with you." Naked frustration darkened his eyes. "This isn't over. You can count on that!"

He turned, stamped to the door, jerked it open and walked out.

Joanna placed a hand against the wall to steady herself, certain that everything that had once held her world intact had broken apart.

"I've got problems, Mike."

Mike looked up from the folders on his desk and scowled at Tony. "Who doesn't?"

Tony slouched on the corner of Mike's desk. "What the hell's eaten at you? These last two days, you've been meaner than a junkyard dog."

"What do you want?" Mike asked coldly.

Tony sighed. "All right, have it your own way. The club's enrollment has dropped."

"I find that hard to believe, when I have more clients than I've ever had."

"The bosses want you to get more. Get my drift?"

"Screw the bosses."

Tony grinned. "My thoughts exactly, only both our jobs depend on keeping them happy."

"The bank happy, you mean?"

"Right."

"Well, I can't take on any more clients," Mike said without hesitation. "Going to school limits my time."

"That's what I told 'em."

"Well, I'm not going to worry about it." Mike leaned back in his chair and placed his hands behind his head. "I can only do what I can do."

Tony slid off the desk with a shrug. "They told me to pass the word to you, so I did."

"Thanks—you did your duty. Now get out of here and let me work."

When Tony reached the door, he turned. "I hope you're feeling better tomorrow."

"Don't count on it."

"I won't," Tony said with a humorless grin.

The second the manager walked out, Mike peered down at the folder in front of him. But the notes he'd taken in class last night might as well be in Greek for all the sense they made.

Letting go of a stinging curse, Mike slammed the folder shut and lunged to his feet, a scowl rearranging his features.

He'd let her get off the hook too easily, he told himself. After what they had shared, she couldn't just toss him out of her life like an old shoe.

"She damn sure did, though."

Speaking to the empty room seemed to have the desired effect. His heart and lungs cleared, and he could breathe again. He walked to the door of his office and closed it, but not before he peered onto the free-weight area packed with men and women pumping iron.

He scratched his chin, finding it hard to believe that the club was short of patrons. Yet he knew that people were fickle and that the fitness business was cyclical. And as he'd told Tony, he couldn't do any more. Management would have to look to someone else to cure their ails.

Mike watched the progress on the floor, then closed his door. Since it was a sure bet that Joanna wouldn't be coming this afternoon, his late time slot was open. He longed to be working out himself or be in the gym across town boxing. Then again, he knew both would be a session in futility.

Joanna had him so torn up that nothing he did or said made any sense. After he'd gotten over the shock, he'd blamed himself for the entire debacle. But he hadn't figured out a way to make it right. Maybe that was impossible. She'd been so angry with him, showed him how little she trusted him. No doubt, his work was cut out for him . . . because he had no intention of leaving her alone.

A baby. They had made a baby.

His heartbeat faltered, and a cold sweat drenched his skin, leaving him weak all over. Before now, he hadn't let himself dwell on that fact. He couldn't ignore it any longer. He had no intention of letting her assume the responsibility of the baby alone, despite her apparent determination to do just that. He could be as stubborn as she was.

It wasn't just stubbornness, though. It was more, much more. Pain knotted his insides. He had fallen in love with her, something he swore he'd never do. He had lowered his shield, allowed himself to be swept away by his own emotions, until she had him snared in a web from which he couldn't get loose.

A baby... his baby. *Their* baby.

He bit his lip. He kept on biting his lip. Only after he tasted blood did he hurry out of the room.

Joanna stared at the computer screen on her desk and read the words and numbers. Everything there made perfect sense.

Automatically, she reached for the switch on the printer and listened to it hum as it printed out the material that she'd been working on since she'd arrived at work at six o'clock that morning.

"Ms. Nash, is the document ready?"

Joanna looked up and smiled at Tammy, one of the clerks in the office. "Yes."

"I'm finished with my other work. Would you like me to distribute it?"

Joanna smiled a relieved smile. "Oh, would you? That would be a great help as I've got to get these other communiqués out for Mr. Granger."

"It's good as done," Tammy said brightly. At the same time she crossed to the desk and reached for the papers.

Once she was alone, Joanna turned back to her work, only to find she could no longer concentrate. Mike dominated her thoughts and her heart. She'd known she was asking for trouble when she'd continued to see him. As for sleeping with him . . . Well, she couldn't even begin to beat up on herself enough for that.

The worst part of the entire scenario was that she'd fallen in love. She propped her elbow on the desk and leaned her head in her hands, but refused to give in to the tears that threatened, although she feared the ball in her throat might choke her.

Had she been too hard on him? She didn't think she had, despite his concern for her health. She guessed what had hurt the most had been his anger, so similar to her ex-husband's. Andy's anger had stemmed from his lack of love, the same as Mike's had. Without love, the foundation of a relationship was weak.

So what else was new? She'd made another error in human judgment. She never did anything by halves; with her it was all or nothing. Even her bad marriage hadn't changed that. It was the way she was.

When she could cope, she'd call her physical therapist and ask him to recommend another trainer. She couldn't face Mike again, not while her emotions were still so raw.

"Ms. Nash?"

She swung around. Tammy stood on the threshold. "There's a man who insists on seeing you."

"Who is it?" Joanna asked with a frown.

"Me."

The sound of Mike's low voice and the sight of his dark head behind Tammy made her stomach turn over with both fear and delight. With the exception of the dark circles under his eyes and the tense lines around his mouth, he looked as good as she'd ever seen him.

Instead of his workout gear, he had on a pair of worn, washed-out jeans and a navy pullover that made him appear rougher than usual. But his eyes, as they swept over her, were anything but rough. They were filled with anguish. She finally managed to drag her gaze away, stand up and walk from behind her desk.

He strode deeper into the room, stopping short of touching her.

"Joanna, I had to see you." His voice sounded unnatural, as if it didn't belong to him. "I've been a miserable SOB."

She swiped at a tear and dug her teeth into her bottom lip.

"Oh, honey, don't cry. I can't stand it."

"I can't help it."

"Are we alone?" he demanded thickly.

She nodded in the affirmative.

He pulled her into his arms and sank his hands in her hair as his mouth came down on hers. He was devouring in his intensity. Momentarily, she moaned and gasped for air.

With her stomach settled somewhere around her knees, she stared up at him, her heart weakening under his smoldering glare.

"Promise me we'll work it out." His voice sounded as if his throat had been dusted with sandpaper.

"Oh, Mike."

"I admit that the baby shook me up and that I acted like a sonofabitch, but—"

She placed a finger across his lips and halted his words. "I was as much to blame as you. I was angry and wouldn't listen to reason."

"So, are you willing to now? All I'm asking for is a little time to adjust."

"All right."

He grinned with his heart in his eyes. "You won't be sorry."

"I'm going to hold you to that," she whispered, lifting her lips to his.

Fourteen

———

Mike stepped out of the shower and heard the phone ring. Securing a towel around his waist, he crossed to the bedside table and lifted the receiver.

"Yeah."

A warm chuckle caressed his ear, upping his pulse. "I certainly hope you weren't expecting anyone important to call."

"She just has."

"You're never at a loss for words, are you?" Joanna's voice held a teasing warmth.

"Not when I'm talking to you."

"What were you doing?"

"Getting out of the shower."

"Oh."

Despite her lack of inhibitions in bed, he knew her face would be red. He laughed. "Wanna join me?"

"I thought you said you just got out," she responded coyly.

He sat on the side of the bed. "Well that's easy to fix. I'd be more than willing to drop the towel and step back in."

"I bet you would."

He chuckled. "Just talking about washing you from head to toe makes me want you."

Her sharp breath rattled through the phone line. "You always want me."

"You do crazy things to my body."

A short silence followed.

"Are you still there?" he asked in a husky voice, feeling the ache in his gut spread to his groin.

"I'm...still here."

He chuckled again. "Well, are you on your way over?"

"You know I'm not. I'm at work."

"That's too bad."

"You're bad."

"Not as bad as I'd like to be. Right now, I'd like to have you under me and—"

"I'm going to hang up before we're both in trouble."

"No, don't hang up," he said. "I'll behave."

"That'll be the day."

"What time can I pick you up tonight?"

"Seven. Are we still going to your friend's club to dance?"

"Yep. That is, if you're up to it."

Another short silence ensued.

"I'm pregnant, Mike," she said softly. "I'm not an invalid."

His grin faded into a frown. "I know, but—"

"I'll see you tonight."

The phone clicked in his ear. He didn't know how long he held the buzzing receiver before he replaced it on the hook. Ignoring the trembling in his limbs, he stood and let the towel drop to the floor.

They seldom talked about the baby, although thoughts of the tiny being they had created hovered at the edges of their consciousness. Joanna seemed content to give him the time and space he needed to come to terms with her pregnancy.

A month had passed since she'd told him. Since then, he'd spent as much time with her as possible. They hadn't discussed their future or the baby's. But he knew that, too, was imminent.

No matter how much time he spent with her, it wasn't enough. He loved her to the depths of his soul, and it wasn't just her luscious body or the way she whimpered when he was inside her. Much more drew him. He admired her sharp wit and mind, yet he found her a complicated mixture of self-doubt and self-confidence.

Despite the fact that he still didn't see himself in the role of daddy, he couldn't stop thinking about the baby.

And the baby was still very much on his mind thirty minutes later when he walked into the club, past the front desk.

"Hey," Tony said, "wait up."

Mike stopped abruptly and swung around.

"Man, are you in a stupor, or what?" Tony demanded. "I hollered at you twice before you heard me."

"Maybe I'm getting hard-of-hearing," Mike said, thrusting aside his agitation at Tony in general.

Tony gave him a strange look, then said, "I just thought I'd warn you that you have a visitor."

"Who?"

"Jesse Barnes."

Mike thought for a moment. "Who's he?"

"He said he was from Ashland Oil in Dallas."

"What does he want with me?"

"He didn't say. Maybe he's looking for a trainer."

"Yeah, sure."

Minutes later, Mike walked into his office and watched as a distinguished gray-haired gentlemen, who looked to be in his early sixties, stood, his hand outstretched. "Jesse Barnes, Mr. McCoy."

"Mike."

"All right, Mike."

"Have a seat."

"Thanks."

Once his visitor was seated, Mike crossed to his desk and eased into his chair. "What does someone from an oil company want with me?"

Barnes smiled around perfect white teeth. "Ah, you get straight to the point. I like that."

Mike waited without comment.

"I have a proposition I'd like to make you."

Mike glanced at his watch. "Without sounding rude, if you can do it in thirty minutes, I'm all yours. After that, I have a client."

"Fair enough."

Mike crossed his arms over his chest. "I'm listening."

"Damn," Joanna muttered as she stared at the snap on her jeans, the snap that wouldn't close.

This would never do, she thought, as she took off the slacks, yanked a hanger out of the closet and slipped them back onto it. Then, chewing on the side of her mouth, she located another pair, one that had been too large for her several months ago.

Only after she had them on and buttoned did she feel a sense of relief. No way was she going to get fat, yet there she was well on her way.

She gritted her teeth and concentrated on finishing dressing. Soon Mike would arrive, ready to go. Tonight would be the first time they had gone dancing, and she was both apprehensive and excited.

She didn't consider herself a good dancer, since she hadn't danced in years. But Mike said it was one of his favorite pastimes, that it was great exercise.

Once her hair and her makeup were intact, Joanna remained in front of the mirror where she placed herself under close scrutiny.

She didn't look fat, at least not to the unknowing eye. That little baby in her womb was hers and Mike's secret, although he hadn't mentioned it. The only thing he'd commented on were her breasts.

"My mother must have weaned me too early," he'd said thickly while fondling a swollen nipple.

" . . . Or maybe you're just male," she'd countered with a catch in her voice.

The memory of that conversation, two nights ago, sent heat flooding though her body. Yet sex between them, as perfect and fulfilling as it was, seemed no longer enough.

She knew she'd promised to give him time to adjust to the baby, to plan for its future, and possibly their future, as well, but she was getting antsy.

Suddenly she placed her hand on her stomach and felt again the thrill that darted through her each time she thought of the miracle growing inside her. She wanted this child so desperately. At the same time, she wanted it to be a part of a real and loving family.

Tears burned her eyes, and she stared hard at her stomach, as if she could see the life growing there. But something else was growing there, too—fear. A gut-wrenching fear that Mike was never going to love her or the baby the way she wanted him to. Battling back a sudden feeling of fatigue, she sat down on the side of the bed and drew a deep breath. If only she were strong enough to let Mike go—now, before she became so dependent on him for her everyday survival that she wouldn't ever get over losing him.

Pushing that thought aside, she stood and checked her makeup, just in time to hear the doorbell chime. Giving in to her excitement, she hurried to the door. "I'm coming."

Mike's eyes rested on her, his mouth twitching, as if aching to explode in laughter.

"Don't you dare say it," Joanna threatened, "or you're dead meat."

"Say what?" he asked innocently. "That you have two left feet."

They had just arrived at his apartment from the country-and-western bar where they had spent the past few hours. Since it was Saturday night, Mike wanted her to spend the night at his place for a change. She'd agreed, feeling at home in his small but spotlessly clean two-bedroom apartment.

She elbowed him hard in the ribs.

"Damn, woman!"

"Serves you right," she said without remorse.

His laughter finally erupted. "For someone who's a mere hundred pounds, you pack a wallop."

"I'll have you to know I weigh a hundred and ten."

Mike tossed his Stetson on the back of the couch. "That's only because of the ... baby."

"True, but maybe I'll hang on to some of that extra weight."

"It wouldn't hurt. I've always said you were too skinny."

She made a face. "*Thin* is the correct word."

"Yeah, you'd think someone as skinny as you could move their feet better."

"I told you I couldn't dance, but you wouldn't listen."

He grinned. "I won't make that mistake again, but it might be too late. Even my boots couldn't protect my toes. They're a bloody mess."

"Funny."

He patted her on the butt. "Park it."

After she sat down on the sofa, she peered up at him. "So do I have to work out tomorrow?"

"Same time, same place."

She groaned. "Doesn't dancing count for anything?"

"Stop your whining. Of course, it counts, but it doesn't take the place of your workouts. It's just an added plus."

She groaned again at the same time she gave him a scathing look.

He caressed her cheek. "Sit tight while I get us something to drink."

"You want me to do it?"

"Nah. You just relax."

She wished she could. Although she'd tried her best, she hadn't been able to completely push aside her depression. It had lingered around the edges of her heart like a thief, tainting the evening's activities.

While they'd had a wonderful time, a wall existed between them, the wall her pregnancy had created. He couldn't even say the "word," she thought with despair.

She'd acted as though she hadn't noticed his hesitation when he'd said the word *baby* a few minutes before. She hated that it bothered her, but it did. It hurt her like a sharp pinch to her tender skin every time it happened—because she knew in her heart that he hadn't as yet accepted the idea of fatherhood.

Suddenly tears burned her eyelids. Determined not to cry, she shifted positions. The unexpected move dislodged a cushion. Underneath was a book.

Joanna picked it up, and seeing it as a means of taking her mind off her heartache, she thumbed through it. Only after she reached the middle did it dawn on her what kind of book it was.

"Oh, dear Lord," she wheezed, her breath damming up in her throat. She shut the book and read its title: *Better Homes and Garden New Baby Book*.

A thrill shot though her, even as she tried to come to grips with what it meant. She knew what it *could* mean. Dare she hope? Dare she hope that maybe he did want the baby, after all? And that maybe the three of them had a future?

"Are you all right in there?" Mike called from the tiny kitchen, an offshoot of the living room. "You're awfully quiet."

Joanna fought for control of her splattered emotions while storing this precious tidbit in her heart to be examined later. "I'm fine. What's taking you so long?"

"I spilled the damn coffee grounds all over the counter. I can't believe my foul language didn't burn your ears."

Her lips curved into a satisfied smile. "My mind was elsewhere."

He muttered something she couldn't understand, but it didn't matter. Her heart was singing a tune all its own.

He sat down beside her a few minutes later, all grins. "You look like a cat who just finished licking a bowl of cream."

She stretched, which drew his eyes to her full breasts.

"You're asking for it." His voice sounded strained.

"What?"

"You know what," he muttered.

Fifteen

—

Their eyes held. Longing robbed Mike of his next breath as he took in her huge eyes and the quivering lower lip.

Joanna opened her mouth, but nothing came out.

Mike saw the moist tip of her tongue, and his temperature shot up. He groaned before hauling her into his arms and burying his mouth against her neck.

"I can't seem to get enough of you," he whispered, his hands touching her. Her skin felt hot underneath her blouse, a hindrance to his growing desire.

"I have the same problem."

He drew back slightly but kept his hands on her shoulders. "So what do you suggest we do about it?"

"Mmm, now let me see. . . ."

He kissed her nose. "You want to play hard to get, huh?"

"I just want to play."

He kissed her then, long and hard.

The instant he heard her answering groan, his arms tightened, and he rained kisses along her neck, her cheek, not stopping until he reached her lips, making them his own again.

A guttural whimper seemed to come from deep inside her as their mouths met. He loved the sounds she made. When one of his callused hands circled a breast, she clutched his shoulders, dug her fingers into the hard flesh.

While their lips continued to devour, slick and quivering, his fingers sought the other breast, touching, massaging until both it and the nipple throbbed.

She shoved her fingers in his hair, outlined his ear with a fingertip. Then finally pulling back, she whispered, "Oh, Mike..."

His lips left hers still aching for more. "'Oh, Mike,' what?"

"I don't remember what I was about to say."

His eyes sparked with amused passion. "It doesn't matter. Nothing matters except burying myself deep inside you. Come on."

They stood and, arm in arm, made their way into the bedroom.

Without taking his eyes off her, Mike urgently disposed of his clothes. The moonlight poured through the blinds, bathing the room in a soft glow.

He stood naked before her. Joanna's eyes widened. "You look like some Greek god," she whispered, a tinge of color staining her cheeks.

"After seeing me naked so many times, I still can't believe you blush."

"I'm not blushing."

"Liar," he said softly, a slight shake in his voice.

Her tongue flicked out and trailed across her lip in a provocative manner. Her mouth glistened.

His blood pressure skyrocketed. "You're asking for it." His words were barely audible.

"Nothing but promises, promises," she teased, the tip of her tongue once again circling.

He swallowed hard while his hot gaze roamed her fully clothed body. "It's your turn now."

Her eyes dropped to the buttons on her blouse and with trembling fingers, she fumbled with them.

He brushed her fingers away. "Let me. My hands are steadier." Only they weren't. They shook with almost the same intensity as hers. He mumbled a curse.

Then he felt Joanna's eyes on him as he slid his callused hands down her arms, pulling off her blouse. Finally her clothes joined his in a pile on the floor and for a moment, he simply stared at her. The moonlight pearlized her taut flesh beginning with her swanlike neck, her dainty shoulders...and her burgeoning breasts starting to swell with milk for his child. For the longest moment, his gaze settled there.

Suddenly he developed the weak trembles; the sight of her nude body was such a stimulus that he wasn't sure if his legs would continue to support him. Still, he couldn't stop his greedy eyes from moving down to her rounded stomach, the dark curls at the apex of her thighs...

He tried to swallow, but he had no saliva. She was the loveliest creature he'd ever seen, and she was his for the taking.

"Love me, Mike," she said achingly.

"With pleasure," he ground out.

But the instant they fell onto the bed, it was her hands that registered claim to him.

"I swear you're some kind of witch. Your hands are doing things to my body..."

"If I'm a witch, then you're a magician."

Her fingers slid over his body in light touching strokes, turning his insides to mush. He was powerless against her.

And wasn't this what he'd ached for, to have her touch him like this, to touch her, to make love forever? Yes, yes, yes, his mind and body cried.

"You're paying me back, aren't you?" His carefully enunciated words came out a muted groan.

Her hands stilled across his lower stomach. "How did you guess?" she whispered.

Their eyes met and held.

He paused for another long moment. "Go ahead, touch me." He barely had the strength to speak as her fingers hovered, teased...

The urgency in his low, rasping voice proved to be the key that unlocked her hands. One surrounded his hardness, then moved to cradle all of him.

He sucked in his breath while the sweet savage foreplay tapped the secrets of his body. At last he couldn't stand the torture a moment longer.

"I want you now!"

"Yes, oh, yes."

Because she was ready, he was able to thrust his hardness into her softness with ease. But once he felt her glove him, he shifted, swinging her on top.

She gasped as she peered into his eyes.

"How does that feel?"

"Different," she whispered.

"But not good?"

"Not...good...just...wonderful." She began to move.

"It doesn't hurt? You're not hurting the...baby?"

She smiled and reached for his hands and placed them over her throbbing breasts. "No, the baby's fine and so am I." She leaned over and placed her lips against his.

He transferred his hands to either side of her buttocks and they began to move together, slowly at first, then with a frenzy.

"That's good...perfect!" he cried, feeling her stiffen in climax as he poured himself into her, the frenzy beginning all over again.

Within minutes, she lay atop him, his arms locked around her, their heart beating as one.

Joanna awakened to the smell of bacon. Her gaze traveled to the clock and saw that it was after eight. But since it was Sunday, she didn't have to move if she didn't want to. Faint rustling from the kitchen alerted her to Mike's whereabouts.

Smiling, she actually pinched herself to make sure she was alive. Then she placed her hand against her stomach and thought about the baby. She didn't know if the sudden gnawing in her belly was from excitement or hunger or both.

It didn't matter; she needed to get up anyway. She'd wanted to mention to Mike the baby book that she'd found buried under the cushions, but there hadn't been a chance. She giggled aloud. They'd been too busy sampling each other's bodies.

This morning would be an even better time, she told herself, getting up and going into the bathroom.

A short time later, she was dressed and wandering into the kitchen, feeling more confident about Mike than she ever had before. Their future did indeed look bright.

"Good morning," she said from the doorway.

At the sight of her, his eyes lighted. "All dressed, huh?"

"And hungry."

He grinned. "You need say no more. Chef McCoy is right on cue."

"How come I didn't know you could cook?" she asked and watched as he set a plate filled with bacon, scrambled eggs and toasted bagel in front of her.

"Surely you don't expect me to eat all this?"

"I wouldn't have fixed it, if I hadn't," he drawled.

She sighed. "I'll try."

"Atta girl."

He joined her then, his own plate heaped high, but he watched her more than he ate.

"Are you satisfied?" she asked, pushing her near-empty plate aside.

He smiled. "Yep. You did good."

"You didn't."

"I guess I'm too tired to eat."

She flushed.

He threw back his head and laughed, only to sober just as quickly. They looked at each other a moment, then both began speaking at once.

"You go first," he said.

"No, you first."

He stood and walked to the window above the sink. She noticed that his shoulders had stiffened. She frowned, wondering what he had on his mind.

He turned, then leaned against the cabinet. "I've been offered another job."

"Is that good or bad?"

"Depends."

Her frown deepened. "I don't understand. You already have a job. Why would you be interested in another one?"

"This one's in Dallas."

If he'd slapped her, she couldn't have been more stunned. "Dallas?" she repeated stupidly.

Mike shoved a hand through his hair. "This guy just showed up at the club yesterday—out of the blue, actually—saying that he'd heard good things about me."

"In Dallas?"

"I found that hard to believe too, at first. But then he mentioned having talked to a mutual friend who I'd helped regain the full use of his limbs. Anyway, this guy, whose name, by the way, is Jesse Barnes, is a VP with an oil company."

When he paused, she jumped in, "What does some bigwig from an oil company want with you?"

His half smile was indulgent. "Physical fitness, that's what. His company, like thousand of others, has invested in a state-of-the-art exercise facility, with the largest indoor track in Dallas, or so he says. Added to that is a comprehensive wellness program used by seventy-two percent of the employees."

"Am I supposed to be impressed?"

He raised an eyebrow. "Well, I sure as hell am. But I'm more impressed that they want me to direct it." He smiled like a child who had waited till the last minute to pull the surprise out of the cookie jar.

She forced a smile. "That's nice."

"Hey, can't you do better than that?"

"What about school?" What about *me?* she wanted to ask but didn't. "I thought you only wanted to work part-time so you could finish your degree."

"I do, but that can wait. That's no longer the most important thing to me."

She looked startled. "Since when?"

"Since I need money."

She shook her head, feeling herself grapple to come to terms with what he was saying.

"Then you *are* interested in the job?"

"You bet."

Her heart sank. "Why?"

"Why? I thought that was obvious."

"Not to me," she said flatly.

"Well, there are strings."

She glared at him. "Get to the point, okay?"

"I'll take the job only if you'll go with me."

"Are you serious?"

"As serious as I've ever been about anything."

"But—"

"Stop stammering," he said with a smile. "I love you. You have to know that. And if you'll have me, I want to marry you."

Joanna was too shocked to speak. Then joy swept through her so strongly that she felt as if she might be having a heart attack. Her prayers had been answered. Wasn't this what she'd ached for, a commitment from him, to her and the baby?

The baby. Her elation twisted into a sharp pain. What about the baby? He never said a word about wanting or loving the baby.

"My God, Joanna—" He broke off midsentence and walked toward her. "Did I say something wrong?"

"No," she said through tear-filled eyes, "it's what you didn't say." She paused and drew a shuddering breath. "What about the baby?"

Sixteen

The room turned almost deathly quiet.

Joanna watched as a myriad of emotions played across Mike's face; she tried not to ignore the clutching sensation in the pit of her stomach.

"Answer me, Mike. What about the baby?" She couldn't gloss over the frantic pitch to her voice, but she didn't care. Her entire future and that of her unborn child were at the mercy of this moment.

Still Mike did not respond. He bit down on his tongue. He bit it again.

"I guess I have my answer," she said without emotion, a feeling of sadness so acute inside her that she felt physically sick. Their bodies had found harmony, but nothing else had. "Your silence says it all," she added weakly.

His eyes followed her. "Where are you going?"

"Home."

"Don't . . . please."

Anger replaced the despair. "Your silence is all the answer I need." She scooted back the chair and calmly rose to her feet.

"Don't go," he croaked.

She twisted around and looked into his gravely tormented features, but felt no pity, just more of that incredible sadness.

"Please, give me a chance to explain."

"What's there to explain?" Her voice was like her insides—dead.

He cleared his throat as if he found it difficult to speak. "I've come a long way toward coming to grips with the baby. But I guess I need more time."

She gave a savage shake of her head. "It's not that simple, and you know it."

"It is that simple," he said, his voice now ringing with urgency. "But you're trying your best to make it complicated."

She grasped the back of the nearest chair in order to hold herself steady. "I'm trying not to make the same mistake. You want *me*, but—"

"I love you, dammit! There's a difference."

"I don't doubt you love me, but that isn't enough." She spoke with deep regret. "You—"

"Joanna."

"Let me finish, please."

He gave a frustrated nod.

"You proposed to me for the wrong reason."

"Love *is* the only reason I asked you to marry me," he countered.

"But only because you love me, you'll accept the baby." She paused, battling the despair raging inside her. "I don't want a man who is crazy about me, but regards the baby as part of the package. I want you to love and want our baby as much as you love and want me."

Mike stood there for a second, his face filled with dark uncertainty. "You don't give an inch, do you?"

"I can't afford to."

"Just a little more time is all I need. Is that asking too much?"

"Yes."

That tiny word seemed to have the effect of a loaded gun fired without warning.

Mike's head snapped back. "So where does that leave us?"

"I think it's obvious. I've been down that road before, Mike, and I don't intend to ever go again." She paused while her heart constricted painfully. "Andy didn't want our baby, and like you, he kept pleading for time. Only that time never came. When Megan was born, he resented her. Sometimes I think he even hated her because she took me away from him."

"Dammit, Joanna, I'm nothing like that animal you married."

Her lower lip trembled, and for a second she tried to force it into a smile. "No, you're not, except where the baby is concerned, and I see one too many similarities."

"That's a damn lie."

Her chin jutted. "Then prove it. Tell me you're as excited about the baby as I am, that you can't wait to be a parent."

Deep furrows crept across his forehead. "You know I can't do that. Not yet, anyway. But that still doesn't mean I don't—can't—love our... baby."

"See, even now you stumble over the word, and the sad part about it is you don't realize it yourself."

"Is there anything I can say to get through to you?"

"No."

He bent slightly as if she'd kicked him in the solar plexus. "Is that your final word?"

"Yes."

"If that's the way you want it," he said harshly, "then who am I to try to make you see reason?"

"Sarcasm doesn't fit here."

His nostrils flared. "Not a thing you're saying fits here either. But if you've made up your mind, then there's nothing I can do. Rear the child by yourself. I don't give a damn."

Silence, sudden and complete, fell over the room. Joanna forced herself to move.

"Where are you going?"

"To get my purse and call a cab."

An expletive singed the air. "You're not calling a cab. I'll take you home."

"Fine."

The instant Joanna walked into her house and closed the door, she slumped against it. Tears scorched her eyelids and clogged her throat.

"Damn him! Damn him to hell," she whispered in a hissing tone, clenching and unclenching her fists.

He'd kept on until she had fallen in love with him, till he had her right where he wanted her. Then, when responsibility time came, he shirked his duty. She should have known better than to trust him. Fool, fool, fool. That was exactly what she was.

She shivered suddenly and tried to move her stricken legs, but it was impossible. They were too feeble to make even the smallest step.

If she could hang on to the sudden twisting, violent anger that possessed her, she just might survive. If not... She shivered again, the alternative too unbearable to contemplate.

A wretched sob tore through her. "Mike," she sobbed.

"Hey, that's the way to do it, champ."

Peyton Weir, Mike's eight-year-old nephew, flashed him a grin. "Wow, Uncle Mike! This is neat."

"Think so, huh?"

"Can we box the rest of the day?"

Mike laughed and tousled his dark curls. "Nah, you'd get too tired."

"But—"

"Don't argue. We'll give it another shot tomorrow. I bet you have some homework to do. Right?"

Peyton looked disgusted. "It's Saturday, Uncle Mike."

"Ah, it is, isn't it?" Time flies, he thought, thinking back to almost a week ago. "Sorry about that. Well, you've worked out enough for today, anyway."

"Are you guys ever going to quit?"

Mike looked up and saw his sister, Martha, standing at the edge of the garage. Widowed, she lived in Longview and was the sole caretaker of a son and daughter. Martha was a nice-looking woman, he thought suddenly, watching the sun play across her features.

"Mom, wanna watch me punch the bag? Uncle Mike says I have real talent."

"I'm sure you do, son." Martha smiled indulgently. "But I'll watch another time, if that's all right. I want to talk to Uncle Mike."

His mouth turned down. "Can I go over to Joey's, then?"

"Yes, but be back in time for supper."

"Okay."

They watched in silence as Peyton hopped on his bicycle and pedaled down the drive.

"He's quite a kid," Mike said, smiling at his sister. "You've done a great job."

"Thanks, but it's been tough." She paused and bit her bottom lip. "I still miss Larry, and it's been three years since his death."

"Why haven't you ever married again, sis?"

"I've never found another man who could fill his shoes."

Mike's face turned grim. "I know what you mean."

"I've made a fresh pot of coffee. We need to talk."

That was what had driven him here after his break with Joanna. Of all his brothers and sisters, he and Martha had been the closest. Since he hadn't been able to stand his own company, he'd called and asked if she'd like a visitor.

"Are you coming?" Martha asked, interrupting his thoughts.

"Shortly. I need to take down the punching bag so you can get your car back in the garage."

"The coffee'll be waiting."

He dismantled the punching bag, but instead of heading straight to the house, he walked to the fence at the rear of the yard and stared at the empty pasture beyond, empty like his life.

He'd told Joanna he didn't give a damn. Those words had haunted him day and night because he did give a damn. Only, he hadn't realized how much until she was no longer a part of his life.

That emptiness inside him was as complete as if someone had taken a knife and gutted him. He despised feeling that way, and he didn't know how to cope. That emptiness brought back tainted memories of his past when he'd approached his daddy, when his daddy had told him to leave him alone, to find something else to do.

God, he missed Joanna and loved her more than he ever thought possible. But did he love her enough to make that ultimate commitment of becoming an unselfish and committed parent?

After wrestling with that question over and over, he still didn't know. And he still couldn't stop thinking about their baby. *His* baby. But what did that mean?

"Mike! Where are you?"

Swallowing a deep sigh, he pivoted and walked toward the house. "Hold your horses, I'm coming."

The second he walked in the back door to the kitchen, Martha reached for the coffeepot and filled a cup.

"Sit," she said.

"Yes, ma'am." His eyes twinkled. "Still the same old bossy sister, I see."

She wrinkled her nose at him, then grinned. "I guess some things never change."

"No, I guess they don't." His face turned dark again.

They were silent for a minute while they sipped their coffee.

"Suppose you tell me what's got you turned inside out?"

He swallowed hard. "It's that obvious, huh?"

"I'm afraid so. Is it that job in Dallas you told me about?"

"No. I've made up my mind not to take it."

"Then your trouble has to be a woman."

"Right."

"Tell me about her."

He looked at her through hollow eyes. "It's over between us."

"Tell me about her, anyway," Martha encouraged softly.

He told her then, as much about Joanna and their breakup as he thought she needed to know.

"I'm sorry, Mike. She sounds like someone I'd like."

"There's more."

"Oh?"

"She's pregnant."

Martha's eyes widened incredulously. "And you let her go?"

He lunged to his feet, his features twisted in agony. "I was scared, scared deep in my gut, and I still am."

"For heaven's sake, why? I've never known you to be afraid of anything or anyone, not even Daddy when he used to unleash his temper on you."

"That's just it. I don't know if I'm capable of loving a child because of Daddy. Hell, we both know he didn't love us, especially me. What if I turn out like him?"

"You won't."

"How do you know? It happens every day."

"That's true," Martha said earnestly, "but you're nothing like Daddy. Besides, you love Joanna, and Daddy never loved Mama. We both know that now."

Mike blew air out of his lungs. "I don't know."

"I do," she said with a smile. "I know you, and I know you have a great capacity for love." Her eyes teared. "If it hadn't been for you, my life would've been much rougher than it was."

"I—"

"Don't you dare deny it. You took care of me, listened when no one else would. And you were there for Abbey and Trina, as well. So don't give me that garbage that you wouldn't make a good parent, because you would."

"I wish to hell I could convince myself."

"Well, you're scared. That's perfectly understandable. Both Larry and I were scared when we had our children. Parenting is a huge responsibility, but that didn't stop us from taking the gamble."

"I tried to explain."

"Did you? Did you really?"

"No, you're right, I didn't."

"Maybe if you had, she wouldn't have been so quick to judge you."

"I don't know."

"Remember when you worked with the United Way through your boxing?"

He frowned. "What does that have to do—?"

"It has everything to do with it. You worked with kids who didn't have fathers, who craved attention, right?"

"Right."

"And how many times did you tell me their sad little faces would light up when you'd pay them special attention?"

"True, but—" He broke off, then slammed a fist in the palm of one hand. "Oh, God, I'm about to do the same thing to my kid, aren't I?"

Martha smiled, then looked up. "Thank God, something finally got through your thick skull."

He'd been to hell and back. He tried to speak, but he simply didn't have the strength. All his vital energy had drained from him. The thought of *his* kid becoming one of those victims turned his stomach. And worse, what if Joanna married, and another man reared his child? No! A sharp pain hammered at him. He wouldn't allow that to happen. The thought of another man's hand on Joanna's swollen belly, and later holding his child, burned his gut.

"Mike?"

He stared at Martha.

"I can see your mind spinning. So what are you going to do about it?"

What was he going to do about it? How was he going to right a terrible wrong? He knew now that he did indeed want his baby; he wanted to share in its life. His pigheadedness and Joanna's stubbornness weren't going to rob him of that. He would make her listen. He would convince her that he wanted them both because he couldn't stand the thought of living without them.

Suddenly he grabbed Martha and gave her a bear hug.

"Hey, you big oaf, let me go!"

Mike let her go, but not before saying, "Thanks, sis, for everything."

"But I didn't do anything."

He smacked her playfully on the cheek. "Yes, you did. You put up with my bad attitude and helped knock some sense into my addled brain."

Martha laughed. "You're right, big brother, I did. And for that I deserve a medal."

"Sorry, you'll have to settle for another kiss."

She laughed again and slapped him on the arm, her eyes sparkling with sudden tears. "Go on, get out of here."

Mike paused at the door, a vulnerable look on his face. "Wish me luck."

"You know I do," she whispered.

He walked out, feeling better than he'd felt in days. Joanna had to listen. She just had to. He wouldn't take no for an answer. Not this time, not ever again.

Seventeen

"**I** think that will do, for the time being, Ms. Nash."

Joanna breathed a sigh of relief, then stood. "When do you think the trial will actually get underway?"

Cameron Delaney sighed. "If I had my way, we'd be in court right now, but you know our justice system..." He let his voice trail into another sigh.

Joanna was quiet for a moment as she watched the federal district attorney stuff papers into his briefcase, then pause to put them in order. He was a small man, with a thatch of red hair, but surprisingly no freckles. Although he had been calm and methodical throughout the procedure, he had a sharp mind. If anyone could nail her ex-boss on fraud and other related charges, it would be Delaney.

He had arrived at her office unexpectedly, saying there were a few things he needed to go over with her.

Her boss had offered them the conference room, and they had just finished.

"We'll need to meet several more times in order to make sure you're prepared," Delaney said before snapping his case shut and looking up at her, his keen eyes piercing.

"I understand," Joanna said, a troubled look on her face. "But what if he wins another postponement?" She spread her hands. "I mean this could go on forever, couldn't it?"

"Very definitely." Delaney's smile was sardonic. "But again that's the American way—hurry up and wait."

"What do you think of our—the government's chance of winning? I know several bigwigs have already been convicted. Are our chances better because of that?"

"Oh, we'll get a conviction—I'm confident of that." Delaney crooked his elbow, then propped it against his briefcase and put his weight on it. "Your testimony is invaluable, as you well know."

A tiny frown marred Joanna's forehead. "What if I don't come through? What if—"

Delaney interrupted. "You'll do fine. Tell the truth—that's all we're asking. In your case, the truth is pure gold."

"I know, but I'll still feel better when it's over."

"Won't we all, Ms. Nash." He straightened. "I'll be in touch soon, and we'll run through another question-and-answer session."

Joanna folded her arms as if to protect herself from some unknown force lurking in the shadows. "Please do. I know what a crackerjack attorney Sam Wise is—" She paused, flushed, then hurried on to say, "Not that you aren't, Mr. Delaney."

He smiled that sardonic smile again. "Think nothing of it. I know Wise, personally. And you're right, he's an SOB, if you'll pardon the language. But I have every confidence in you as well as our entire defense. Mr. Hancock is not going to be free much longer to pollute our streets."

"That sounds good."

He smiled briefly, then latched onto his briefcase and strode toward the door. Once there, he turned around, the smile still intact. "Don't you worry. You'll do just fine."

"Thanks."

He nodded. "I'll be in touch. Meanwhile, take care." He had his hand on the knob and had the door open, when he swung back around. "Nothing out of the ordinary has happened, has it?"

"You mean to me?"

"Yes. I take it, the police still have you under surveillance?"

"As far as I know. But to tell you the truth, I've stopped looking for the plainclothesman." She shrugged. "I told Detective Mason I don't need that service, but he wouldn't listen to me."

"I'm glad. It's better to be safe than sorry, Ms. Nash."

"I know, but I feel—oh, I don't know, maybe the word's guilty."

"Forget it. Most of the time it's good citizens like us who can't get help from the law, so take advantage of it. Anyway, this is a very important case. It's different, and the country will be watching it closely. So we—*you*—can't be too careful." He paused. "You'll let me know if anything changes."

"I promise."

"Good," he said shortly. "Again, I'll be in touch."

When she was finally alone, Joanna felt as if she'd been beaten with a baseball bat. She'd dreaded preparing for the forthcoming trial and now that it had begun, her apprehension deepened. Climbing into the witness chair and airing her ex-boss's dirty laundry did not appeal to her. But because she had an obligation to the taxpayers and her own conscience, she would do it and do it to the best of her ability.

Deciding that she had lollygagged long enough, Joanna gathered her notes and headed for the door, only to stop. The smell of fresh-brewed coffee tantalized her senses.

Seconds later, she had a hot cup and was sitting in the executive chair, staring out the window. The day was lovely. A perfect day for a picnic, she thought with a pang, a picnic with someone you love.

Hot tears pricked the back of her lashes. "Stop it, Joanna," she hissed aloud.

Unfortunately, her harsh words didn't have the desired effect. When she had severed her relationship with Mike, she had been sure she could cope. After all, it was just another dark time in her life. She had overcome so much already that she'd been convinced she could overcome losing him, too. It hadn't worked quite as planned.

She was more miserable than she thought possible. She ached for Mike, literally. Not since she had lost her daughter, had she felt that deep, gaping hole in her heart. She missed his smile, the twinkle in his eye, his big body when he took her with his sweet, savage artistry.

The tears tickled down her face, but she didn't bother to flick them away. Maybe a good cry was what she needed, even if she was at work. Yet the gut-cleansing sobs wouldn't come. If only she didn't miss him so much. If only she was half as strong mentally and physically as she'd thought she was.

The future—well, that didn't bear thinking about. Her free hand went to her stomach where she drew sudden comfort from the life that was growing there.

Was she up to the challenge of single parenting? No, she wasn't, but it didn't matter. Somehow she would muddle through, just as she always had.

Suddenly she thought of Kim and her parents and felt better. Kim was as excited about the baby as if it were her own. And even her parents, after the initial shock had worn off, hadn't disowned her. She hoped that once the baby was born, they would come around entirely. But if they didn't, then she'd manage without them as she had so often in her life.

"Joanna."

She looked around. Tammy stood hesitantly in the doorway. "I hate to disturb you, but you had a phone call from Detective Mason. He wants you to go to the police station immediately."

Joanna stood, her heart plummeting to her toes. "Thanks, Tammy. Call and tell Mason I'm on my way, please."

"All right."

What on earth did *he* want? Something of grave importance, she knew or he never would have called her downtown. She refused to borrow trouble. Once she cleared her leaving with Calvin, she'd know soon enough.

A short time later, Joanna found her way into the police substation. She was shown into the detective's stark office.

"Thanks for coming, Ms. Nash," he said, pointing at the chair in front of his desk. "Have a seat."

"Thanks," she murmured.

Mason sat down behind his desk and eyed her carefully, then smiled. "I guess you're wondering why I called you to come down here."

"As a matter of fact I am," Joanna said evenly, although her insides were tight as coiled springs.

"I have good news, that's why."

Joanna blinked. "You do?"

"That's rare, I know."

"I didn't mean it like that," she hurried to say.

He waved a hand through the air. "It's all right if you did. It's the truth and we both know it." He paused and scratched his head.

Tense and upset, Joanna turned her gaze away.

"Anyway," he went on in a complete businesslike tone, "I didn't call you down here to talk about the injustice of justice."

Mason smiled as if he'd made a joke. Joanna smiled in return, although hers never reached her eyes. Suddenly she felt more exhausted than ever. She wished she were at home on the couch.

"The mystery surrounding your hit-and-run has been solved."

She thought she hadn't heard him correctly. "Pardon?"

He smiled again. "We have the culprit in custody."

"You do?" she managed to get out, knowing she must sound like a fool.

Mason stood, then crammed a hand down one pocket. She heard him fiddle with his keys. "The parents of a teenage boy walked into the station this morning and told us their son had run you down."

Joanna felt her face drain of color while her head spun.

"Are you okay, Ms. Nash?"

Joanna heard the detective's voice come from a long way off, but was powerless to respond. Only after he'd repeated his aversion several times did she recover and say, "Sorry... I'm just stunned, I guess."

"It's not a pretty story."

"What happened?"

"Seems that he and his girl, whom he'd just taken home, had had a tiff. To help him cope," Mason added with a sneer, "the boy drank several beers."

"Oh, my. I can imagine how his parents must feel."

"No, you can't."

"No, I guess I can't. What will happen to him?"

"That's up to the judge. I hope he throws the book at him."

"How old is he?"

"Sixteen."

"Oh, my," Joanna said, thinking about the child she carried and the awesome responsibility to make it a good citizen.

"The D.A. plans to try him as an adult, which is good."

"His poor parents," Joanna said again. "How did they find out?"

"He confessed, actually."

Her eyes widened.

"Yeah, that's a switch, isn't it?" Mason shook his head. "These teenagers today, as a rule, are something else. Anyhow, his mother said he'd been behaving strangely and that he'd been in trouble at school. Finally they sat him down for a heart-to-heart. That's when he spilled his guts."

"So it was an accident, pure and simple?"

Mason snorted. "Oh, it was an accident, all right. But the pure and simple part, I'll have to pass on." His eyes narrowed into hard pinpoints. "He could've killed you, you know. So don't go feeling too sorry for him. He has to pay for what he did."

"You're right. He does."

"I'll keep you updated."

Joanna held out her hand and smiled. "Thanks for everything, Detective."

He grinned then dropped her hand. "Even the hovering plainclothesman?"

"Even him." A sudden twinkle appeared in Joanna's eyes. "But I was right, after all. I told you I wasn't my ex-boss's target."

"You're lucky. But it's still better to be safe than sorry."

"You're right, of course. And I want to thank you for taking care of me."

"You're welcome." Mason turned his head to one side and scrutinized her closely. "Are you sure you're all right? You're awfully pale."

"I'm sure."

But she wasn't. Joanna found this out after she got home. Nausea sent her dashing to the bathroom. Later, after she'd lost the contents of her stomach, she sat on the couch, relieved that the day was nearly over and that she could go to bed.

She had showered and eaten a bite. Both had made her feel much better. Yet her mind remained in a turmoil. She couldn't stop thinking about the teenager who had hit her. Idly she flicked on the TV, but since there was nothing she wanted to watch, she reached into a basket beside the sofa for her Lamaze book.

She sat back to read, but her mind wouldn't settle. With her mouth set, she stared at it, only to suddenly freeze. Instead of seeing the title of her book, another took its place. *Better Homes and Garden New Baby Book,* the one Mike had hidden.

What did that mean? She'd never gotten the chance to question him. Her heartbeat turned wildly irregular. What did his having the book prove—that he cared more than he had let on, much more than she'd thought?

Joanna's eyes darted around the room while her heart continued to beat at an abnormal pace. Had she been too quick to jump to conclusions, too quick to condemn him?

Her mind rehashed the events of that day, painful as they were, recalling how she'd not given him much of a chance to talk, to tell her how he felt. There were different stages of love. Could it be that his just hadn't quite progressed to the stage of hers. If so, was that a crime? No, she decided.

She bent slightly, then rocked forward. In his own way, he'd tried to tell her that, but she hadn't been in a mood to listen. Out of stubbornness and pride, she'd been willing to deprive her child of its father.

God help her. What an utter fool she'd been. Not only that, but she'd found him guilty by setting herself up as judge and jury.

Her breath hung suspended, and she didn't move. However, her brain continued to churn with reborn possibilities. Dare she try it? Dare she try to make amends?

The instant Joanna pulled against the curb in front of his apartment, she saw him. Braking suddenly, she sat still and watched.

The dying sunlight silhouetted him as he stood at the rear of his Jeep, the tailgate lifted. He tossed a bag inside. Had he accepted that job in Dallas, with plans to make a new life for himself that didn't include her and their baby? Her heart split and her hopes faded. If he was leaving, it served her right. Still that thought didn't lessen the pain.

As though he felt himself under observation, he swung around. Joanna clenched the steering wheel while he stood unmoving, like a picture in a frozen frame. The only indication that he'd seen her was the narrowing of his eyes.

Then he began walking toward her. Joanna held her grip on the wheel, fearing if she so much as moved, the gash in her heart would widen. But when he reached her car, Joanna's reflexes took over, and she let down her window.

They stared at each other for an electric moment. Then they both began to talk at once.

Only after they realized they were both apologizing, did they stop.

Then Mike said with controlled anger, "If you don't get out of that car, I'm going to crawl in there and get you."

Crying joyously, Joanna thrust open the door and flung herself in his arms.

Eighteen

"I love you," Mike mumbled over and over against her earlobe, her neck, her pliable lips.

"And I love you."

Joanna's clothes lay on the floor next to his. Their lips never parting, he swung her naked body into his arms and carried her to the bed.

His hands immediately cupped her swollen breasts and enticed the nipples to instant erection. After bathing the valley between them with his tongue, he trailed a path down her stomach, scorching her flesh wherever he touched. Her eyes fluttered shut. Her head lobbed sideways. A moan escaped her lips. She grabbed at him, crying for the full effect of his steel muscles. The tightness inside her finally erupted, and she arched her hips wildly.

"I was afraid I'd never be a part of you again," he whispered.

"I was afraid, too."

Another deep groan escaped her at his sharp penetration, then a deeper, more precious sensation took over. She sank her nails into his taut buttocks and urged him on.

His thrust never wavered, not even when they cried simultaneously, "I love you!"

He kissed her quivering lips and with great care wiped the tears from her cheeks. When the tears subsided, and she raised her gaze to his, the odd brilliance in his eyes stole her breath. She smiled as he pulled her into the crook of his arm and covered a breast, still throbbing with desire.

"What time is it?" she asked in a drowsy, sated tone.

"Does it matter?"

"No, not really."

"Well, I'll humor you, anyway. It's a few minutes after twelve."

"Oh, Mike, is this real? Are you real?"

Moments after she'd lunged out of the car and into his arms, they had made their way into the house, with only one thought in mind—loving each other, making up for the time they had been apart.

Now was the first opportunity they had taken to unburden their hearts.

His hold on her tightened. "What do you think?"

"I'm afraid to think, for fear I'll find you a dream."

"I'm no dream, my darling. We're together, and I don't intend to ever let you out of my sight again."

"Ever?"

He squeezed her closer. "That's right. Any objections?"

"None whatsoever," she whispered. "These last few weeks were too painful. I wouldn't want to relive them."

"I was a fool for letting you walk out on me in the first place."

"You weren't alone. My past experience had me so blind-sided that I couldn't see your pain for my own."

"And now?"

"I know deep down that you want our baby." She heard his audible sigh of relief as she went on. "But I also know you're scared—as well you should be." She paused, struggling to find exactly the right words. "When I got a taste of what it was like without you, I forced myself to rehash our last conversation, word for word. Too, I kept seeing the torment in your face. I realized suddenly that you were hurting as badly as I was, but you just didn't know how to voice that pain and uncertainty."

"I never meant to hurt you. And as you say, deep down I wanted our baby, only I—"

She placed a finger against his lips, silencing him. "It's all right, I understand."

His tongue flicked out and licked her finger. Then he spoke, his voice sounding unnatural. "What made you change your mind? Something had to trigger those thoughts."

"The book."

"Book?" He sounded as confused as he looked.

"Ah, stop playing the innocent."

Mike continued to look confused.

"The *Better Homes and Garden New Baby Book.*
Does that ring a bell?"

His face turned red, and he looked sheepish, almost
embarrassed. "Yep, as a matter of fact it does."

"Care to tell me how you came to have it in your
possession."

"I bought it at the grocery store. I saw it and before
I knew what was happening, I was paying for it along
with my broccoli."

"And did you read it?"

"Parts of it."

"Oh, Mike, I should've known when I saw that book
that you cared more than you'd admit, only—"

"Hey, don't beat yourself up any more. We both
screwed up. Let's leave it at that and go on from here."

She touched her lips to his chest. He jumped, and she
smiled.

"See what happens? You only have to touch me, and
I go berserk."

"Same here."

They were silent for a while, each enjoying the
closeness of being together.

"Have you gotten a new trainer?" he asked at last.

Joanna cut him a look. "Now, what do you think?"

"I think, no."

"You're right."

"So, we're back in business."

"Uh-oh, I think I know what you're trying to tell
me."

He chuckled. "Right you are."

"You mean I have to start working out again?" She groaned.

"Whining doesn't become you, my darling."

Her hand aimed for his rib.

He trapped it. "Oh, no, you don't. My ribs can't take any more of your—uh, punches." She blushed, and he laughed outright. "Anyway, violence will get you nowhere," he added. "So yes, it's back to the grindstone."

"But what about the baby?"

"No problem, if the exercise is done with sound judgment. The baby'll love it. After all, he's a chip off the old block."

"You're impossible," she said breathlessly, just before his lips sank onto hers for a hot kiss.

Finally she asked, "What about the job in Dallas?" She had dreaded asking this question. While she wanted the best for his career, the thought of uprooting and starting over was disturbing.

"Would you mind so terribly if I took it?"

Although his tone was even, she heard the uncertainty in it and knew she was being tested. "Actually, I thought you already had. When I saw you pitch that bag into the Jeep, I was sure you were on your way to 'Big D.' And, no, I wouldn't mind, if that's what you really want."

He rested a hand on her leg. "You're something else."

"Love does that to you," she murmured huskily.

"Yeah, it does." He propped his chin on her head. "Mmm, did I ever tell you I love the way your hair feels and smells?"

"A hundred times."

He laughed. "Well, you'll be glad to know I turned the job down. I guess when I talked it over with Martha—"

"Who's that?"

Amusement evened out his voice. "My sister."

"Oh."

His laugh deepened. "You were jealous."

"I wasn't jealous."

"Yes, you were."

"Okay, so I was jealous. But back to your sister."

"She's great, actually. I can't wait for you to meet her." He was quiet for a moment. "What about your parents?"

Joanna sighed. "I have no idea. You can't tell about them. But I think they'll be pleased, especially when they find out I won't be rearing the baby alone. Who knows, maybe becoming grandparents again will mellow them."

"Miracles happen."

"I know—we're one," she said.

"That we are, my darling. And so is our baby."

He placed a hand over her stomach. Glassy-eyed, she watched him.

"First thing on the agenda, after we're married—"

She made a gasping sound, stopping him short. His gaze met hers in a probing stare. "Married. Oh, Lord, that's right. We do have to do that."

"Damn straight we do. No child of mine is going to be born a bastard."

She heard the fierce note of possessiveness in his voice, and her heart thrilled anew. "You were saying after we're married—"

"That we'll start your workouts again."

She pursed her lips. "I was thinking you were going to tell me something exciting."

"I want you in shape for labor."

"All right. But there could be a hitch in our plans. The S & L trial is due to start soon. The assistant D.A. came to see me, and discussed the case."

"Don't worry—we'll face it together."

"I have some other news."

"Shoot."

She told him about the teenager who had run her down.

"Well, I'll be damned. You said all along that you didn't think it was related to the case. And you were right." Mike's eyes hardened. "I hope to hell they throw the book at that kid."

"Those were Mason's exact words. It's a shame, though. I feel for his parents."

"You're right, it is a shame, especially when our child will be a teenager one of these days."

"A baby is a big responsibility, but we can handle it, can't we?"

"You betcha."

"I've been thinking. I'd like to take a leave of absence from work and stay home for a while."

"I'd like that, too," Mike said cautiously, "but whatever you want to do is fine with me. I know how you feel about your job."

"I love it, no doubt about that. But I love my two boys a lot more."

He drew back and grinned widely. "A boy, huh? Who says?"

"Me."

"Well, a little girl, who looks just like her mom would suit me just fine."

"Oh, Mike, I'm so happy."

"Me, too," he said, leaning and placing his lips against her stomach. "Me, too."

Epilogue

Six Months Later...

"That's my girl. Breathe."

"I'm breathing!"

Joanna's gasping cry cut into him, but he couldn't let it get to him. He wouldn't lose his nerve now. She needed him, and he wasn't about to let her down.

He drew a deep breath, but when it came out a quiver, he knew he was headed for trouble. He had to get a grip on himself. He mopped his brow and quickly continued his soothing instructions.

"Breathe deeply, love."

Joanna's breath swished in and out.

"Great, honey. We're about there." Mike transferred his anxious gaze to the doctor. "We are, aren't we?"

"Soon, Mike, soon. Keep up the good work, both of you."

"Mike!"

"Doc, do something! She's hurting."

"Not for much longer. The head's in my hand."

"Oh my God, oh, my God." Mike thought he'd lose the contents of his stomach. Both fear and excitement rendered him almost useless. But again he couldn't let her down. "Push, honey, push."

Joanna pushed at the same time her cry rented the air. A split second later, there followed the sound of a wailing baby.

"Michael Scott McCoy."

"He's something, isn't he?" Mike mused, sitting beside Joanna's bed a short time later, the baby nestled in the bend of her arm.

"He's perfect."

Mike leaned and kissed her, then whispered, "I love you."

"You want to hold him?"

Only after Mike had the infant in his arms did he realize his face was saturated with tears. "Ever see a grown man cry?" he asked, his eyes on Joanna.

"No, but it's all right." Joanna reached up and touched his cheek. "It's not every day a man watches his son being born."

Mike responded by kissing the face, a tiny replica of his.

"Isn't he beautiful?"

Mike rolled his eyes. "I'm not sure I like hearing you refer to my son as 'beautiful.'"

"Now, if that doesn't sound like a chauvinist, I don't know what does."

Mike swatted her playfully on the behind. "I confess."

They lounged on the bed on a Sunday morning two months after Michael had been born. This time was precious. With Mike's finishing his schooling and with plans in progress for the sports-medicine clinic, his days were long and full, which didn't lend him as much time with his son as he would've liked.

"But he is beautiful, isn't he?" Joanna peered at the baby between them. "He looks exactly like you."

"I'll admit, I couldn't deny the little rascal, even if I wanted to."

Her eyes turned anxious. "You don't want to." Although a question mark was absent from the end of the sentence, one was there nonetheless.

"Oh, Jo, don't you know how much I love you and our son?" Mike's voice was thick, his eyes passionate as they dwelled on her.

Her features took on a joyous glow. "Of course, I know, but I guess I never get tired of hearing it."

"And I'll never get tired of saying it."

The baby whimpered.

Mike bent over him nervously. "What's wrong with Michael?"

Joanna smiled. "He's hungry, that's all."

"That's my baby," Mike said, placing his palm on his son's head as Joanna uncovered her breast for him to nurse.

The infant's lips attached themselves to her nipple and sucked.

Joanna flinched visibly.

"Does that hurt?" Mike asked, his eyes dark with suppressed passion.

"A little, at first. It's such a shock when his mouth latches onto my nipple."

"Like father, like son."

She blushed. "You're awful." Then she turned to him, her heart in her eyes, to see the yearning in his own gaze.

By the time the baby finished nursing, he was sound asleep. Joanna lifted him into Mike's arms. Moments later Michael was on his back in the crib. Joanna's upturned face was wet when Mike climbed back into bed into her outstretched arms.

"I love you," he whispered, claiming the breast that his son had nursed.

Joanna gave in to the loving warmth that flooded through her, clinging to him. "And I love you, for always."

* * * * *

SILHOUETTE® Desire®

HAWK'S WAY

HAWK'S WAY—where the Whitelaws of Texas run free till passion brands their hearts. A hot new series from Joan Johnston!

Look for the first of a long line of Texan adventures, beginning in April with THE RANCHER AND THE RUNAWAY BRIDE (D #779), as Tate Whitelaw battles her bossy brothers—and a sexy rancher.

Next, in May, Faron Whitelaw meets his match in THE COWBOY AND THE PRINCESS (D #785).

Finally, in June, Garth Whitelaw shows you just how hot the summer can get in THE WRANGLER AND THE RICH GIRL (D #791).

Join the Whitelaws as they saunter about HAWK'S WAY looking for their perfect mates... only from Silhouette Desire!

SDHW1